# The Critters

## *Exploring the Shenandoah!*

**Barbara Banks**

llustrated by: Rossnelly Salazar

# PUBLIC NOTICE

**WARNING** to Parents and Children:
Many critters in this book are naturally wild
animals. Wild animals may carry diseases
and may bite or attack. You should not pet,
play with, or attempt to tame a wild animal.
Wild animals should be left in their natural
habitat. The Critter Family Series is a
fictional story and is written for your reading
entertainment, enjoyment, and learning to
separate fact from fiction.

Text, Cover and Illustrations
Copyright(s) © 2020 by Literary Promenade

Illustrations by Rossnelly Salazar

ISBN -  978-1-952311-03-1     (Paperback, Color)
ISBN -  978-1-952311-04-8     (Paperback, B&W)
ISBN -  978-1-952311-05-5     (eBook)

Library of Congress Control Number 2020908154

Published by Taxiway Publishing
Oak Hill, VA

# Dedication

For my husband,
Chuck,
who is always there for me!

I greatly appreciate his enthusiastic support and dedication to the book series and for being my sounding-board and editor of my initial drafts. He dedicated so much time and refined his computer skills to self-publish this book series. I am so grateful! It felt like ole' times working with someone who is used to flying by the seat of his pants (He recently published <u>Low and Fast: Memories of a Cold War Fighter Pilot</u>)!

# Other Books

## By Barbara Banks

### The Critter Family: The Fun Begins!
Published February 2020

### The Critter Family: To Wyoming and Back!
Published September 2020

# Future Books

### The Critter Family: Untitled!
Coming soon

# Trademarks

Millicent Mink™
Amber Cat™
Hal Thoroughbred™
Stretch Greyhound™
Rona Rabbit™
Mako Kai Ken™
Dallin Duck™
Casey Cardinal™

Abbie Alpaca™
Darcy Pony™
Tizzy Pug™
Scampy Squirrel™
Cara Cardinal™
Fifer Fox™
Roxbury Raccoon™

# Characters

Chris (Dad)    Natty (Mom)

Wendy (working daughter) Allie (college daughter) Todd (11)    Megan (9 ½)    Brody (8)

- Granddad (Natty's dad)
- Nana  (Natty's Mom)
- Hank    (Alpaca rancher in Shenandoah, Maggie's husband, Ryan's dad)
- Maggie  (Alpaca store owner, Hank's wife, Ryan's mom)

 Ryan (visiting parents Hank and Maggie)

 Ed (Shenandoah camper)

- Madeline (Ed's wife) (Shenandoah camper)

# Contents

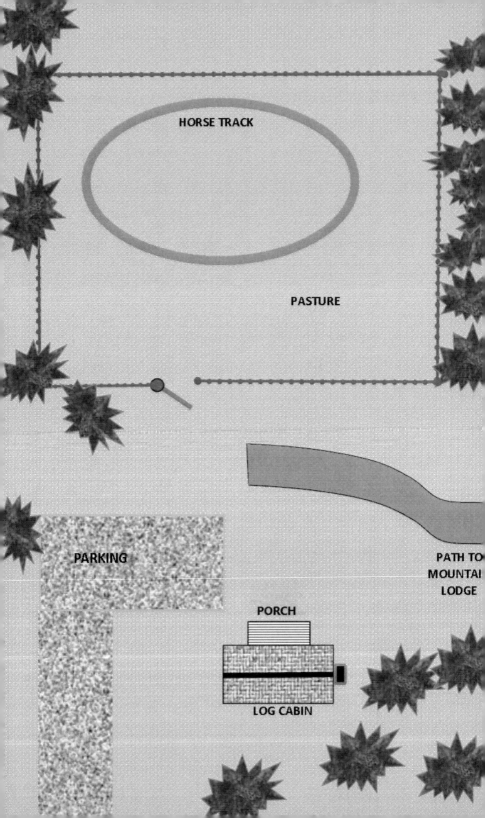

# Chapter 1 - The Hummer

**W**endy led the way in her blue SUV for a country vacation in the Shenandoah Valley. As she drove out of the driveway and down the road, Wendy saw Paul and his wife working in their front yard. Wendy honked her horn and waved.

Wendy's dad, Chris, was following her in his truck and noticed that the neighbor waved to Wendy. He decided to stop and meet them. Chris honked his horn and motioned for Wendy to stop.

Chris said to Natty, "Let's introduce ourselves to the neighbors. It'll take a minute. We haven't met any of the neighbors yet. Wendy has met these folks, probably on her walks with Mako."

Chris and Natty jumped out of the truck.

Chris said, "Hi, we're the new neighbors. I just want to introduce my family. We are heading for the Shenandoah Valley right now."

Paul said, "I'm Paul and this is my wife, Lori. I met Wendy and Brody during one of their morning walks."

Chris said, "We can talk more when we get back. We're planning a gathering later this summer, and you're invited. We do need to get on the road. We'll be back in a week. Nice meeting you!"

Paul waved to Brody and said, "Sounds good! Looking forward to it. Have a safe trip. By the way, how many animals do you have there?"

1

Chris said, "We moved here with three pets and added five more. They're amusing! See you in a week."

The two-hour drive to the Shenandoah went quickly. Megan and Brody played a game with highway signs. They started by finding a word starting with A, then moved on to the next letter in the alphabet. When they reached Z, Brody exclaimed, "Z is impossible! We'll never see a word with Z in it."

Just then, Megan yelled out, "ZONE! Construction Zone! I win!"

Chris pulled up to the cabin which got the critters excited! Chris had arranged to stay in a friend's cabin for the week in the Shenandoah Valley. He thought that staying in a cabin located at the base of a Mountain gave them easy access to the Valley and the Mountain Lodge.

Hal Thoroughbred™ started to whinny in the horse trailer and thought, "Smell that fresh air! This is fun!"

Mako Kai Ken™ was in Wendy's SUV thinking, "I want out! How about you, Stretch?"

Stretch Greyhound™ pushed against the door and thought, "Mako, I'll race you to the pasture as soon as this door opens!"

As the doors opened, Mako and Stretch tumbled out of the car in their rush to race for the pasture. Amber Cat™ slipped out of the car behind Mako.

Amber thought, "I have a porch with a swing and rocking chairs! I want to rock. I can lay in the sun and watch everyone in the pasture!"

Chris gathered everyone in front of the cabin and said, "The cabin has quite a few rooms and there is a fenced pasture area for the critters. Todd, Wendy, Allie, and I will carry the luggage and groceries into the cabin.

Then I want to visit the Mountain Lodge to check out the area. Anyone want to come with me?"

"I do, I do" were the responses!

"Okay!" Chris said. "Wendy, Todd and Mako! We'll head for the Lodge as soon as we get settled. Oh, first rule. No one will be outdoors later than sunset. Not dark, but sunset! I want all the critters put down for the night by sunset so that we aren't dealing with other animals coming down from the mountain. Okay?"

Natty turned to everyone else and said, "Okay! Well, let's be quick to settle in so that we can explore! I'll open the windows for the cabin to air out. Allie and Brody, please help get the critters settled. Megan, can you help me? You can assign bedrooms by putting people's luggage in any room that you don't want! Then, come back to the kitchen and tell me what you want for supper. We will eat what you want tonight!"

Brody said, "I would have helped you, Mom, if I knew that you would cook what I wanted to eat!"

Mom said, "Aw, Brody. Just be quick in volunteering the next time!"

Allie quickly said, "Come on Brody, let's go to the pasture. Let's count the critters to see if they're all here. Let me know if one of them is missing!"

Brody said smartly, "Okay, boss lady!"

Allie shook her head laughing, "You got that right!"

Chris and the others headed for the car to visit the Mountain Lodge.

When everyone was back at the cabin, Chris said, "The Mountain Lodge is really nice. I met an alpaca rancher. He invited us to visit his ranch. He said that his son, Ryan, has a very fine horse. Ryan would like his horse to spend time with Hal. I'm going to check out

Ryan's horse tomorrow. Now, the other part of the deal that we made will wait until tomorrow."

Natty replied, "You have secrets! Does this rancher have a name?"

Chris looked puzzled and said, "Hmm, I don't remember his name!"

Wendy came in from the pasture and said, "It's hard to keep an eye on Millicent Mink™. Her dark fur is hard to see, and the sun is going down. Should I put her in a crate in the pasture with the others or in the truck bed?"

Allie said, "Todd and I will help Wendy. We'll put Millicent Mink in the truck bed for the first night along with Dallin Duck™ and Rona Rabbit™. When we're done, Todd can help me set up my new hammock that I got on our trip to the Outer Banks in North Carolina. I'll never forget our trip to Kill Devil Hills where the Wright Brothers flew their first flight! I wish that I could have watched them trying to fly!"

Todd added, "Dad, you're a pilot. I'd like to learn to fly. Can I take flying lessons somewhere?"

Dad answered, "We'll look around when we get back home. You need to be 14 years old to fly a glider and 17 to take a private pilot's flight test. You can start reading about things taught in ground school like the difference between types of airplanes, airplane controls, and aerodynamics, plus effects of altitude, air pressure, wind, temperature, and aircraft weight. There's a lot to learn. We can visit a library. Remember, you'll be learning to drive a car when you're 16."

"Wow!" Todd exclaimed. "I can't wait to be 16!"

Dad laughed, then said, "Okay, everyone. I'll check on the critters one last time and turn the pasture lights on.

Finish what you're doing so that we can eat and talk about things to do in the Valley."

Everyone drifted back to the cabin to eat, then moved to the living room to talk. Mako, Stretch and Amber laid in front of the fireplace to listen.

Chris said, "When we were at the Lodge, I picked up a map of local hiking trails. There are more pamphlets up there about local events. We can make another trip up there and ask at the front desk about the area."

Natty rose from her chair and said, "Oh, I better call my folks. Remember, they called when we were leaving home. I'll sit on the porch swing to talk."

A short while later, Natty came back in the living room and said, "Well, we're going to have company this week. Granddad and Nana are passing through here on their way to the beach. They should be here in a few days. It's time for bed. Tomorrow is an exploration day."

Todd, Megan and Brody raced up the stairs.

Then the grumbling started. "I didn't want this room!"

"My window faces the road and there's nothing out there to see!"

Chris yelled, "Take it up with Megan. She picked your rooms. Call Mako and Stretch upstairs."

Things quieted down but that didn't stop the whispering between bedrooms that night!

Everyone woke up early the next morning when the neighbor's rooster crowed. Allie got up quickly to head to the pasture to brush Hal and then walk, trot, canter, and gallop him for exercise. Wendy and Megan walked Mako and Stretch. Chris and Todd prepared the critters' food and placed it on the cabin porch. Natty cooked breakfast, filling the country kitchen full of smells from biscuits, gravy, and omelets.

Brody ran to the pasture and climbed up to sit on the fence to watch Hal. He yelled, "Hey Allie! Hal is a racehorse, not a show horse! Hal probably doesn't like what you're doing to him!"

Allie waved her hand at Brody as if to say that she heard him. Then Allie kept up with Hal's exercises.

Hal looked over at Brody and whinnied.

Brody yelled, "Hah, see Allie! Hal agrees with me!" Brody jumped down off the fence and raced back to the cabin to eat breakfast.

Casey Cardinal™ swooped down over Brody's head barely missing him. Casey thought, "Brody, you're a funny kid! I'm watching you!"

During breakfast, Allie told Brody, "Listen, little man! Before a thoroughbred horse races, it learns different maneuvers for control. Hal needs to stay in good shape even if he is retired because he stays healthier that way. Besides, he loves to run! That's why Hal and Stretch are such good buddies. They both love to run!"

A vehicle pulled up to the cabin just then.

Chris heard a horn and said, "That must be Ryan. Hey, why didn't Casey Cardinal warn us? Where is he anyway? Well, let's go meet Ryan."

Chris yelled, "Hi Ryan! We have a great day today. Meet the rest of my family. Natty, this is Ryan."

Ryan said, "Hi, I'm happy to meet you. Let me introduce you to Moonstruck."

Before Ryan moved his horse, a white, fluffy, young alpaca stood up and stepped out of the horse trailer.

Natty cried out, "Well, who is this?"

Chris replied, "This is the other part of the deal!"

Ryan explained, "The alpaca was part of the trade for allowing Moonstruck to spend time with Hal. I've wanted a racing horse nearly all my life. When Chris told my dad about your critter family, this seemed like the perfect trade. My dad has award-winning alpacas on his ranch. Dad's alpaca herd is getting large, so Chris and my dad struck a deal to give a young alpaca to you."

Natty smiled and said, "Now I have my own alpaca! Alpaca fiber is soft and strong for knitting. Thank you!"

Ryan continued, "Alpacas are calm, friendly animals and hum when they're curious, bored, or afraid. You heard her humming. Each alpaca has a different humming sound. When a group of alpacas are together, they sound like a chorus! She'll make a short, sharp whiney sound when she senses danger. If she alerts to danger, check what's happening. She may even spit if she's scared."

The alpaca was surrounded by curious critters staring at her.

Dallin Duck™ waddled up to the alpaca, sat down by the alpaca's front legs, looked up, and quacked, "What are you supposed to be? You have a long skinny neck and are fuzzy all over. Why don't you have feathers like me?"

The alpaca thought, "How did you get all those colored stripes? None of you look like me. I'll learn what you are. But you don't scare me. Besides, you seem to like my being here."

Natty added, "We need to name her."

Allie said, "How about Abbie Alpaca™! She has a cute grin. She can calm down the critters."

The alpaca was surrounded by curious critters.

Wendy added, "It won't be hard to remember Abbie Alpaca if I can wear something from her fur, like a hat!"

Ryan turned to lead Moonstruck to the pasture.

Chris said, "We'll introduce Moonstruck to Hal. I'll put the other critters in the cabin or in the horse trailer for the night. They're amused with Abbie Alpaca."

Chris yelled, "Todd, can you give me a hand to round up the critters?"

"Coming Dad!" Todd answered.

Chris and Natty walked Ryan back to his truck.

Ryan explained, "My dad started the ranch over thirty years ago raising cattle and selling grass-fed beef. At that time, not many farmers identified their products as grass-fed. Now it's more common. Ten years ago, Dad decided to expand his herd to include alpacas. Now he and my mother have a small store with alpaca fiber products like hats and scarves. If you have a chance to visit the store, you can talk to them about how they take the alpaca wool and spin it into fiber."

Natty replied, "I'll plan to stop over in two days!"

Natty thought for a minute, and then asked, "Ryan, is it possible for you to take Abbie Alpaca back to your ranch for the night? She had an opportunity this afternoon to meet the other critters. You could bring her back tomorrow and then take her back to the ranch tomorrow night. When we stop over in two days to see the alpaca store, we can bring her back for good."

Ryan agreed saying, "That will work. Besides, I like visiting these critters. They're fun to watch! I made friends with Mako already at the Lodge."

Natty replied, "While you and Chris are talking, I'll walk Abbie around to get familiar with the place."

Natty walked Abbie Alpaca around the cabin pointing out things to her. Natty led Abbie over to the front porch. Abbie climbed three steps and sat down on the porch, watching the critters in the pasture.

Natty yelled to Ryan, "She wants to stay!"

Ryan answered, "I'll come and get her!"

Ryan and Chris walked over to the porch.

Ryan said, "Come on, Abbie, it's time to take a ride. You'll be back to join them tomorrow."

Abbie Alpaca started to hum as she walked back to Ryan's truck. Abbie walked into the horse trailer and sat down, folding her legs under her body.

Mako looked puzzled and thought, "How did she do that?"

Mako and Stretch watched Ryan drive away but quickly forgot Abbie as they raced back to the pasture!

Allie said, "Casey Cardinal flew off this morning. Has anyone seen him today?"

"Nope, he flew the coop!" laughed Brody, as he tried to do cartwheels in the grass. Then he jumped up, cupped his hands to his mouth and began yelling, "Casey! Casey Cardinal, where are you?"

A while later, Casey flew by and he wasn't alone. Chris said, "It looks like Casey found a friend! If Casey's friend stays with him, we'll have to name it!"

Natty said "Chris, if it's bright red, it's a boy. If it's light in color with red patches, it's a girl. So, Casey found a friend! He didn't waste any time"

Allie helped her dad set up the horse trailer for the critters to sleep in.

Chris said, "Mako, Amber, and Stretch can spend the night in the cabin with us. Millicent Mink, Rona Rabbit, Dallin Duck, Casey Cardinal, and now Casey's friend need space in the horse trailer. The smaller cages will hold the critters for the night."

Allie said, "Really, Dad! Don't you think that Casey and his friend can sleep in the trees? Besides, try to get them into the truck! Where is Millicent Mink anyways? I haven't seen her for a while."

Dad looked puzzled saying, "She'll show up!"

Chris turned on the pasture lights and went inside.

The night was peaceful until Hal whinnied loudly during the night. Chris jumped out of bed and went outside on the porch to look. Chris turned on the outside porch light. The flood lights on the pasture lit up a large area. Chris noticed bright eyes near the pasture fence at the base of the mountain.

"Hey, get out of here!" Chris yelled to scare it off, then returned to the cabin and said to Natty, "I hope that we don't have any trouble. There's a wild animal sitting outside the pasture fence. It might be a fox and it could spook Hal and Moonstruck."

Natty replied, "What should we do?"

"Not much we can do other than keep the lights shining on the pasture area. Hopefully, that's enough to keep the fox away from the horses." Chris sighed, thinking about the critters' safety adding, "I brought my shotgun on this trip for protection from wild coyotes. Hopefully, I won't need it."

While everyone was sleeping, Chris lay awake thinking about the horses.

Ryan drove up to the cabin early the next morning. Casey Cardinal wasn't around again to warn them!

Abbie looked around for her new friends thinking, "I don't know why Ryan brought me back here, but I like riding in the horse trailer. Some of them look strange, but I really like that horse. He's friendly!"

Ryan said, "It's pretty obvious that Abbie likes it here. I forgot to mention that alpacas are friendly with children, dogs, cats, and horses. Did you notice that Mako and your greyhound move closer to Abbie Alpaca when she's here? Abbie is trying to figure out the rabbit and the cat playing in the grass."

Natty said, "Ryan, that's Stretch Greyhound, Rona Rabbit, and Amber Cat. If you're around long enough, you'll remember their names! Abbie Alpaca will fit in the critter family. Each of the critters seems to find a friend in the group. I wonder which critter Abbie will make friends with. Rona and Amber spend time together; Millicent Mink and Dallin Duck spend time around our pond; Mako and Stretch run around together; and now Casey Cardinal found his own friend which we have yet to name!"

Allie added, "Ryan, have you seen Millicent Mink around? Has anyone really noticed where Millicent spends her time since we've been here?"

Ryan said, "No, I haven't seen her."

Natty said, "Come sit on the porch and we can talk."

Chris and Ryan sat in the two rocking chairs talking and watching the horses in the pasture.

Ryan noticed that Megan, Todd, and Brody were sitting on the pasture fence watching the critters. Ryan said, "You mentioned that you just moved from New York. I've always wanted to visit the big three horse racetracks in Kentucky, New York, and Maryland."

Chris said, "I don't have much experience around horse racetracks. My background is in aviation. Racing horses was my grandfather's dream. He gave Hal to us when Hal retired from racing. He believed in keeping retired racehorses in good shape but most people don't spend much time once they retire their horses. My grandfather had a special feeling for Hal and wanted Hal to enjoy being around young people and stay active. My grandfather still has racehorses in New York."

Natty reached for her knitting as she sat on the porch swing. Natty said, "You may have an opportunity to meet my folks in the next day or two. They are driving here after a vacation in Canada and want to visit. They haven't seen the kids for a while."

Ryan replied, "That would be nice to meet them. Well, I better round up Moonstruck and head back."

Chris opened the gate to the fenced pasture area for Ryan to get Moonstruck and take her home.

Ryan was loading Moonstruck in the horse trailer when Natty said "We'll stop by tomorrow to visit the alpaca store. I want to meet your family and bring Abbie Alpaca back!" Just then, Abbie backed away from Ryan as he led her to the horse trailer.

Natty said, "Abbie wants to stay, Ryan."

Ryan turned and patted Abbie Alpaca's head and said, "Come on Abbie, you'll be back tomorrow. Let's go see your old friends!"

The next day after breakfast, Chris took all the critters into the fenced pasture area with Hal.

Chris arranged them in a circle and said, "We're going to get Abbie Alpaca. Mako, you're in charge. Stretch, you help Mako. Keep all the critters in the fenced pasture area until we get back from Ryan's place. We won't be gone long."

Chris walked across the field, locked the gate, and headed to the truck.

Chris told Natty, "Brody and Megan can ride in the truck with us. I'll take the horse trailer to bring Abbie Alpaca back. Wendy can take Allie, and Todd with her in her car to shop at the alpaca store, then drive up to the Lodge and look around for a hiking trail."

When they arrived at the alpaca ranch, Ryan's parents greeted them and walked with them to the alpaca store. Wendy admired the beautiful alpaca garments and purchased a pair of warm alpaca slippers. Then Wendy, Allie, and Todd headed to the Mountain Lodge.

Chris said, "You have an ambitious son, wanting to own a future racehorse. I wish Ryan a lot of luck."

Ryan's dad, Hank, said, "We can shear Abbie Alpaca when she is ready. We can teach you how to shear an alpaca. Just gather the fur and bring it to our ranch. We will wash it and use a spinning wheel to pull threads from the fiber. Then you'll have Abbie's yarn for knitting."

Natty said, "I'd like to learn to use a spinning wheel too, if I could. I'll find time to come back."

Chris and Natty were leaving the store when Hank said, "Maggie and I would like to give you something, if that's alright! We have an animal who seems unhappy because Abbie Alpaca is leaving. We were wondering if you would consider taking them as a pair."

Natty said, "What are you talking about?"

Hank said, "A Shetland Pony. Darcy Pony™ and Abbie have been friends since Abbie was born."

Chris chuckled, saying, "What do you think, Natty? What's one more!" Hank led Darcy over to Abbie and they got excited.

Natty said, "How can I say no! Look at them!"

Brody overheard them talking and yelled, "Yippee! Now I get to ride my own pony! Allie has Hal!"

Chris and Natty were saying goodbye to Hank and Maggie when Ryan began putting Darcy Pony in the horse trailer. Natty turned to watch and nearly bumped into Abbie Alpaca. Abbie leaned over toward Natty and stared in her face, then brushed against her nose.

"You just got your first alpaca kiss!" Ryan said laughing. "Abbie Alpaca must like you already. Alpacas are attracted by someone's smell, mostly their breath!"

Natty said, "Oh, dear!"

Turning to Chris, Natty asked, "How many critters do we have now?"

Chris laughed and mumbled, "Who's counting!"

As Ryan guided Abbie Alpaca into the horse trailer, Millicent Mink walked out from around the alpaca herd. Ryan laughed. "Sorry! It was my fault. Millicent must have slipped into my horse trailer with Abbie a couple of days ago. I noticed Millicent here yesterday after I brought Abbie back. I should have called you, Chris."

Chris said, "Millicent Mink must have been having a good time over here. Now she can ride along with Abbie Alpaca and Darcy Pony! Come on Brody, Megan. It's time to go! We can visit the herd some other time."

As Chris, Natty, Megan, and Brody were driving away, Chris waved to Hank, Maggie, and Ryan and yelled, "It was fun!"

15

## Interesting Information about the Alpaca

The alpaca has been around for thousands of years in South America, Asia and Africa. It came to the United States and Canada in the early 1980s in small numbers. Now there are over 20,000 on private farms. The alpaca is easy to feed because it eats mostly hay and grass.

The alpaca is smaller than a llama. Over half of the world's alpacas live in Peru, South America, in the mountains at high altitudes. It is not a working animal. An alpaca is raised for its special coat. The alpaca coat provides fleece fiber that is strong, silky, smooth, soft, warm, and better breathing than other materials. The fiber tends to be water-resistant and flame resistant.

The alpaca has interesting personality traits. It lives in herds and is very social. Each alpaca has a recognizable face and usually has a cute grin. It can be very curious, alert, calm and friendly, or very quiet. The alpaca can calm others around it. The alpaca communicates through body language. It swishes its tail sideways when it's happy.

Each alpaca has a different-sounding hum. When the alpaca is in a group, their combined hums sound like a chorus. The alpaca may be affectionate and nuzzle your cheek. It might allow you to pet it if it's friendly.

The alpaca can snort when another one is too close to it; grumble to warn each other; cluck to show that it's friendly; scream loudly if it's being attacked; or screech like a bird to scare an opponent. The alpaca might spit if it feels afraid or threatened. It can spit as far as 10 feet away, but it doesn't usually spit at people.

The Alpaca can live up to 25 years.

## Abbie Alpaca
In ***The Critter Family: Exploring the Shenandoah!***,

Abbie Alpaca™ is a quiet and happy critter who has been friends with Darcy Pony since Abbie was born. Abbie shows the Dunn family that she is happy by her frequent humming. She quickly makes friends with Hal, Mako, and Stretch. Abbie is very curious about other critters like Dallin Duck and Rona Rabbit. Abbie is curious about their different looks and they don't move as fast or as far as the other critters. Abbie is used to seeing other alpacas in her old herd.

Abbie likes Natty. Abbie surprises Natty by nose rubbing her. She likes to sit with Natty on the cabin porch as she watches the other critters run in the pasture.

# Chapter 2 - The Jumper

Chris listened for any noise coming from the horse trailer as he drove back to the cabin from Hank's ranch.

Chris said, "Did you hear that? Did that sound like humming to you? It must be Abbie Alpaca."

Brody said, "Better get used to it, Dad!"

Wendy, Allie, and Todd walked out to meet them as the truck approached the cabin. Todd helped take Abbie Alpaca out of the horse trailer, then Darcy Pony.

"Where did you get the pony?" Allie asked. "Don't tell me Hank gave you another critter, Mom?"

Brody interrupted saying, "It's my pony!"

Chris laughed, "Hank said that Abbie Alpaca and Darcy Pony have been close friends. Hank asked if we could keep them together. Mom and I agreed."

Natty turned to Allie and said, "We found Millicent Mink! She slipped into Ryan's horse trailer two days ago and has been over at Hank's ranch playing with the alpaca herd having a great time!"

Millicent Mink heard her name and came bouncing out of the horse trailer.

Millicent thought, "They don't know how good I am at hiding in the horse trailer or that I went to the racetrack with them or that I watched Hal run!" Millicent bounced around as if she were laughing at her secrets!

Chris said "Come on, Darcy Pony. You and Abbie Alpaca will be in the fenced pasture area with Hal."

Chris unlocked the gate and led them over to Hal and introduced them.

Hal thought, "Are they visiting today or staying? Guess I'll find out tonight and see if they're still around!"

Hal whinnied to welcome them and thought, "I never saw a short horse! Did you come with Abbie Alpaca? This pasture is quiet so you better get used to it. It's good to have company even if I have to look down at you."

Chris noticed that Mako and Stretch charged out of the field. Chris was tired of chasing critters today, so he left them alone and walked back to the cabin.

Todd yelled, "Look, Abbie Alpaca and Darcy Pony are racing around the pasture in circles! That got Mako's attention. Mako and Stretch came running back to the pasture to run with them."

After they stopped running, Darcy Pony thought, "I know that I'm short, and sort of look like Hal. But I'm strong and can jump."

Darcy Pony was being inspected by the critters. Mako and Stretch just stared at her. Mako walked around her but didn't get close. Stretch didn't seem to care much.

Hal thought, "I can get used to Darcy Pony but her mane is a mess! Wonder who's going to brush that mess."

Chris called out to Hal, "Hal, you're having company tonight. Darcy Pony and Abbie Alpaca will be spending the night in the pasture. I'll turn on the pasture lights to scare off any animals coming down from the Mountain."

Chris turned on the flood lights which were pointed toward the fenced pasture area. Chris whistled and called out, "Mako, Stretch, come here!"

Once inside the cabin, Mako and Stretch rested in front of the fireplace.

Chris turned back to his laptop computer to search the Internet to learn more about Shetland Ponies.

Chris said, "Hey Natty, listen to this! A Shetland Pony like Darcy Pony is a strong and energetic critter. Darcy should be able to carry a lot of weight. Ryan told me that Darcy can jump over a 6-foot fence and is very handy in show jumping and pony events. That gives me an idea! I'm going to try something tomorrow."

The next morning, Chris walked out to the pasture area carrying a saddle.

Chris thought, "Darcy Pony seems happy here. Let's see if I can get this saddle on her."

When Chris was done cinching up the saddle on Darcy Pony, Chris said, "Allie, want to ride Darcy?"

Allie was quick to say, "No! I'm used to riding Hal. You can, it's your idea, Dad!"

Brody came running out of the cabin yelling, "Hey! I get the first ride on my pony!"

Darcy stood still while Chris helped Brody get up on her back. Darcy wiggled a bit and thought, "Where did he get this saddle. Maybe it's not the saddle. Maybe it's just too tight but it doesn't feel good."

Darcy Pony settled down and started to walk. Darcy noticed that Hal and Abbie Alpaca were following her.

As Darcy Pony approached the gate, Chris called out, "Natty, bring Rona Rabbit to me. This will help Rona and Darcy become friends."

21

The critters saw Darcy Pony giving Brody a ride with Rona Rabbit and thought, "Darcy is fun!"

Brody yelled, "Look at Casey Cardinal watching us."

The ride ended and the critters scattered.

The fox showed up late in the afternoon. It walked out from the trees and watched the critters play in the pasture.

Natty walked around the pasture to make friends with Darcy Pony and Abbie Alpaca just as Ryan arrived.

Chris and Natty walked to the fence to join Ryan.

Ryan said, "How's everything going now that Darcy Pony is here? I want to tell you about how useful Darcy has been for Mom. Dad used to put a blanket and two buckets on Darcy. Darcy would walk with Mom when she was berry picking. Darcy is very patient to go berry picking with Mom. Berry picking is not a fast job!"

Natty said, "I'm glad that you mentioned berries. I need to look for berry bushes around our new home!"

Ryan continued telling stories, "We entered Darcy in a jumping competition at the County Fair last year. She just needs some practice if she is going to win a ribbon."

Chris asked, "If Darcy Pony were to practice jumping, how high should we plan to start her?"

Ryan said, "Start at three feet. She jumped out of my Dad's fenced area to get into the neighbor's field after their horses, and the fence was at least four feet high."

Ryan pointed to the base of the mountain and said, "I see that you have a visitor over there by the fence."

"That fellow keeps showing up at night watching Hal and any other critter in the pasture!" replied Chris. "So far, he hasn't done anything but watch."

Ryan said, "Well, just a warning. Keep a watchful eye on him because those fellows can be unpredictable."

The next morning, Allie, Todd, and Brody got up early to brush Hal and Darcy Pony and to feed the pasture critters. When they arrived, Abbie Alpaca was with Hal.

Todd ran back to the cabin yelling, "Dad, Darcy's missing! She's not in the pasture or around the cabin!"

Chris and Wendy ran out of the cabin to search for Darcy Pony. Wendy asked, "Ryan said that Darcy jumped Hank's fenced area to get to the neighbor's horses. Why would she jump when she has Hal and Abbie Alpaca?"

Wendy continued, "Let's search for clues to see if Darcy Pony jumped the fence. Let's walk all around inspecting the fence."

Wendy paused, then yelled, "Dad, look at this! The fence has a big gouge on the top!"

Chris inspected the fence and said, "I don't know why Darcy Pony would jump the fence last night, but she must have had a good reason. Seems she may have gone into the tree area leading up the mountain. Todd, run and tell Mom that we are driving up to the Mountain Lodge. I'll meet you both at the truck."

Chris, Todd, and Wendy jumped into the truck and headed up the road to the Mountain Lodge. When they arrived in the parking lot outside the Lodge, they saw the most unusual scene.

Chris exclaimed, "This is incredible! I've never seen so many deer walking around the parking lot and several more walking up the road. The deer must be used to being around people."

Wendy and Todd got out of the truck to search around the deer herd and saw Darcy Pony standing beside a fawn.

A pair of eyes watched Wendy from the bushes. It was the fox!

Chris got out of the truck and called to Darcy Pony, "Come on, Darcy. Hal and Abbie Alpaca are waiting for you. Did the fox scare Abbie last night?"

Chris led Darcy to the truck and said, "Oh no! I forgot the horse trailer. Wendy, Todd, stay here with Darcy until I drive down the mountain to get the trailer."

Chris walked over to where Darcy Pony had been standing and then looked over at the fox in the bushes.

Chris said to the fox, "What are you watching in our pasture, fellow? Do you just want to make friends?"

The fox lowered his head thinking, "Am I in trouble? I don't want to scare them! He has a friendly voice, maybe it's okay for me to come out."

The fox came out of the bushes and walked to Chris.

Chris thought, "The fox seems like he's looking for a home, and maybe needs friends."

Chris said to the fox, "If you want to make some critter friends, you'll have to go back down the mountain to the fence. Darcy Pony has had enough excitement for one night. Maybe it was you that she followed last night. I don't know yet."

Chris jumped into the truck to head back down the Mountain to get the horse trailer.

Chris yelled out the window, "I'll be right back. Have fun with the deer! Oh, I forgot to warn you. Don't get close to the deer. You might pick up a deer tick which is dangerous. And don't name any deer or it will have to come back with us!"

Chris looked in his rear-view mirror in the truck and laughed. He saw Wendy taking pictures of the deer with her cell phone camera with Todd posing by the deer!

Wendy turned to Todd, watching him stare at Darcy Pony among the deer and said, "Todd, I'm going into the

25

Lodge to see if I can pick up any information about events in the Valley. I'll be right back. If Dad returns before I'm back, call me."

It didn't take long before Chris returned with the horse trailer. After loading Darcy Pony in the horse trailer, Chris, Todd, and Wendy rode down the mountain to the cabin.

Allie and Megan ran to the truck and asked, "Did you figure out why Darcy Pony jumped the fence?"

Wendy said, "We think it was the fox. We found Darcy Pony in the parking lot outside the Mountain Lodge with a herd of deer, standing by a fawn. The fox was in the bushes watching them."

Chris added, "A fox can hook its paws over the wires of a chicken coop and climb fences as if they were ladders. I wonder why this fox didn't climb the pasture fence or jump over it? A fox can jump 6 feet or higher."

Wendy exclaimed, "Darcy Pony must have seen a pair of shining eyes outside the fence. Darcy sensed that Abbie Alpaca was scared. Abbie might have started spitting if she sensed a threat. Darcy could see a pair of eyes outside the fence because the flood light shined in the pasture at night. Darcy ran across the pasture and jumped the fence toward the pair of eyes. She chased the fox through the trees and up the mountain side until she got to the Lodge. What did we find by the Lodge? The fox, Darcy, and a lot of deer. I have to be right about this, folks!"

"You have to be, Wendy!" Todd said teasing her.

Brody ran to the truck to meet them.

Brody said, "Is Darcy Pony alright? Can I ride her?"

Todd got out of the truck and said, "Relax, Sport. Give Darcy a chance to settle down after last night!"

Brody said, "Okay, I'll get her some food. That should be enough time for her. Then I can ride her."

Todd said, "Wait Brody! How would you like to do some heavy work right after you ate? I think you need to wait awhile."

Brody said, "Okay, then I'm taking Abbie Alpaca for a walk. Maybe Megan can come with me. We can walk up the road toward the Mountain Lodge."

Brody yelled, "Hey, Megan! Want to come for a walk with me and Abbie? I don't want to go alone. We can look for berry bushes and flowers. Then we can ride Darcy Pony later today."

Megan ran out of the cabin and said, "Brody, let Abbie Alpaca lead the way. I want to watch her."

Abbie Alpaca walked slowly down the path. She stopped to look back at the pasture to find Darcy Pony.

Abbie Alpaca started to hum and thought, "It's fun to be out of the pasture. If my alpaca friends were with me, we would run around. Brody and Megan would have a hard time catching us. But my friends aren't here!"

Megan said, "Abbie, where do you want to go? Why am I talking to Abbie? She won't answer me!"

Brody laughed, "Boss lady! Alpacas don't talk!"

Abbie Alpaca thought, "Let them laugh. But I'm going to start sitting on the front porch with Natty. I like hearing her talk to me. She'll trim my fur so that I don't get hot this summer. Then she can knit things with my fur. I'm turning back to the cabin. I wonder if Megan and Brody will notice!"

Natty was on the porch and called, "Dinner time!"

Natty turned to Chris and said, "You need to go to the pasture after dinner and check Darcy Pony. If she spent much time around that deer herd by the Mountain

Lodge, you need to inspect her for deer ticks! Darcy gets brushed in the morning along with Hal but we shouldn't wait until then to check her. Brody has started riding Darcy, and I don't want any of the kids getting a deer tick bite."

Chris replied, "Okay, I'll ask Todd to help. He can use a flashlight to help check."

## Interesting Information about the Shetland Pony

The Shetland Pony is the strongest of all the different horse and pony breeds and able to carry over a hundred pounds. It is one of the smallest breed of horses. The Shetland Pony came from Southern Europe and was later taken to Scotland. The Shetland Pony developed in the harsh conditions of the Shetland Isles off the coast of Scotland.

The Shetland Pony is a very intelligent animal and has a good-natured temperament. A Shetland Pony can be stubborn if it is not well-trained. It has a short, muscular neck, short legs, and a stocky body. It has a heavy coat and a long, thick mane and tail to deal with cold and windy weather. Shetland ponies are a variety of colors. The American Shetland has a very different look, lighter in color, than a Shetland pony today in the United Kingdom.

The Shetland Pony was originally used as a work animal pulling carts and plowing farmland. It was used as a pack horse in the middle of the 1800s for work in underground mines. Today it is used for many purposes. It is seen at fair grounds giving rides to visitors, at horse shows giving rides to children, and at petting zoos. They are even used by child jockeys to race in annual events.

A Shetland Pony lifespan is 30 years or longer.

## Darcy Pony

In ***The Critter Family: Exploring the Shenandoah!***, Darcy Pony is a good friend to Abbie Alpaca and becomes good company to other critters in her new family. Darcy is protective of Abbie. Darcy's strong legs make her a good jumper of fences. Darcy sensed Abbie's fear of the fox so she jumped the pasture fence to chase the fox away.

Darcy is a strong pony and can carry heavy loads. She likes to keep Abbie company and to keep Maggie company when she goes berry picking. Now, Darcy enjoys carrying Brody and some of the critters for a ride. Darcy has found her place in the critter family as a protector and a worker to carry heavy loads.

# Chapter 3 – The Comedian

Todd and Megan woke up early before the rooster crowed! They tiptoed down the stairs and went outside. They raced to the pasture and climbed the fence to sit and watch Hal, Abbie Alpaca, and Darcy Pony early in the morning.

Megan said, "Let's get the critters out of the truck and bring them here."

Todd yelled, "Race you!"

Todd and Megan jumped off the fence and ran.

Megan whispered, "Be quiet opening the tailgate. Look at them! These critters are awake and ready to run around."

Todd and Megan raced back to the pasture with Rona Rabbit, Dallin Duck, and Millicent Mink following them.

As they reached the fence gate, Brody yelled from the porch, "Why didn't you wake me!" Brody ran to join them on the fence.

All three of them sat on the fence watching the critters when Allie and Wendy came out of the cabin to brush down Hal and Darcy Pony.

Wendy said, "What are you three doing up so early this morning? Granddad and Nana should be driving here today. Probably early this afternoon, so Mom might need help with breakfast getting the cabin ready for them."

Brody jumped off the fence and started running to the cabin, yelling, "If I get there first, maybe she'll make whatever I want for breakfast!"

Megan laughed and yelled, "Good luck, Brody."

Everyone was getting an early start in the country. Chris even had a good night. He didn't stay up late to keep an eye on the pasture because the fox didn't come back.

Natty made breakfast just like Brody wanted, omelets with biscuits and gravy. Everyone was eating breakfast when a vehicle drove up.

Natty got up to look out front and said, "Where is Casey Cardinal? I wonder who this is. It's Granddad and Nana! They're early. I'll see if they've had breakfast yet. Todd, can you help your dad with their luggage?"

After all the greetings and hugs, Granddad said, "Is there a chance of getting some breakfast? We left really early this morning and didn't stop along the way."

Natty said, "Come on in. We were just starting breakfast."

After breakfast, Nana continued her story. "We had a nice drive here from Ottawa. It took us two days. We had so much fun and made some friends. After deciding to spend two months driving around Canada to see Quebec, Toronto, and Ottawa, we decided to head south to the beach for a while before we go home."

Brody said, "Canada, what's that? Another country or something?"

Nana laughed and said, "Yes, Brody. Maybe later, we can show a map and some of our pictures to you. After our early rise and drive, I'd like to sit on the porch. Would anyone like to join me? Thank you for the delicious breakfast, Natty!"

Natty said, "Let's take our morning coffee outside."

After everyone was sitting and talking for a while, Granddad got up and said, "I want to show you something that we brought with us."

Nana smiled and said, "You're going to love this!"

As Granddad walked to the car and reached into the back seat, a different kind of bark came out.

"What was that?" Brody yelled, running to the car.

Granddad said, "Let me introduce you. We haven't named her yet. Thought you might like to help us do that. We met some folks in Quebec who had a Pug. They loved their Pug so much that they recommended one to us. So, we decided to wait until we got back in the United States and stopped in New York to add one to the family."

Nana added, "Isn't she a darling!"

Megan said with a smile, "Let's wait until we see what she's like. Then tonight after dinner, we can decide what to name her. Okay? Everyone needs to keep their names a secret. It'll be more fun that way."

Nana said, "That's a clever idea. I like it. Let her run. She needs to stretch her legs."

Chris added, "There are a lot of critters for her to make friends with. Look at her racing for the pasture. Wow! She just crawled under the fence rail. Wonder how the others will react to that burst of energy."

Brody said, "I'm going to the fence to watch."

Todd and Megan ran after Brody to beat him to the fence. Once up on the fence, the kids were clapping and yelling things at the critters. Hal wanted nothing to do with the Pug so he broke out into a trot around the pasture. Mako and Stretch ran alongside Hal. Millicent Mink and Amber decided to make friends with the Pug.

The Pug noticed Rona Rabbit and Dallin Duck and walked over to them.

The Pug stopped and stared. The Pug thought, "I wonder if they'll play with me. But they are just staring at me. They're not moving. They're boring!"

The Pug waited a minute, then went back to Amber Cat and Millicent Mink. It didn't take long before the Pug got tired of just running around, not really knowing anyone. The Pug decided to crawl under the fence rail and run back to the porch.

Granddad picked her up, and said, "I think I'll take her for a walk. Anyone want to join me?"

"I'll join you!" said Chris and Allie.

Chris said, "Let's follow the path toward the Mountain Lodge. This road gets pretty steep so let us know when you want to turn back."

Granddad said, "The road isn't the problem, this active critter is hard to carry. I'll set her down so that she can follow us."

When they returned from their walk, they joined Natty and Nana on the porch.

Nana said, "I'd like to take a walk with Wendy. She isn't around much anymore now that she's moved away and working. I'd like to visit with her before she heads back home. We're heading south tomorrow but we'll be back this way before we go home, so I'll have more time to talk to you later, Natty."

Wendy said, "Nana, how far do you want to walk?"

Nana replied, "You lead! I need the exercise."

Everyone had nice walks around the cabin area. There was a lot of forest area and patches of flowers. The day passed quickly. Everyone was back at the cabin for dinner. After dinner, Brody laid on the floor resting when the Pug laid beside him and put her face in Brody's face.

Megan said, "Brody, she likes you! Now is a good time for everyone to suggest a name for the Pug. Who wants to go first?"

Chris said, "I like Peppy."

Natty said, "I like Polly."

Nana thought and said, "What about Lilly? She has a light tan color to her."

Just as everyone started calling out names, Granddad yelled, "Tizzy. She's always in a Tizzy!"

Megan said, "That's it. I like that. Tizzy!"

The Pug heard the name Tizzy and started to bark, apparently agreeing.

"Tizzy Pug™ it is!" said Nana.

Granddad yawned and said, "We need to get to sleep if we are driving tomorrow. I hate to leave because it's so quiet and restful here. But we're driving to the beach."

Megan asked, "What beach are you going to?"

Nana replied, "We don't know. We are just heading for the coast and stopping when we find a place that we like. We love exploring!"

Megan showed Granddad and Nana to their room for the night. Megan led Mako, Stretch, and Brody to their rooms and said, "Try to be extra quiet tonight. They have a long drive tomorrow."

The sun had set so Chris and Todd went to the pasture to round up some of the critters to take to the truck for the night. Chris made one last check on the pasture. All was quiet once again. No fox in sight.

35

The next morning after breakfast, Granddad asked, "Would you like to keep Tizzy here while we're at the beach? Better yet, do you want to make Tizzy a member of your critter family? She gets along well with all of them. You don't have to give us your answer now. She would make a good addition to your family."

Megan said, "Can we? Oh, Tizzy Pug is so cute, and funny. I would take care of her. Can we, Mom and Dad?"

Brody exclaimed, "I will help Megan take care of Tizzy. I will, really, I will!"

Natty was the first to say, "Alright, she can stay. But you two need to keep an eye on her and train her to stay close by. We've already had Millicent Mink then Casey Cardinal wonder off. Tizzy is so active that it may be hard to keep an eye on her. So, you two figure it out!"

A truck horn sounded. It was Ryan driving up just as Granddad and Nana were walking to their car. Ryan jumped out of his truck and came to meet them.

Ryan introduced himself, "Hi, I'm Ryan. I live just down the way. It's so good to meet you! Chris and Natty are new friends of ours and now have Abbie Alpaca from my dad's herd."

Granddad said, "So that's where you got that beautiful alpaca, Chris! We wish that we could see your alpaca ranch. I'm sure raising alpacas is interesting."

Granddad and Nana said their goodbyes with hugs and kisses all around. Granddad called out from the car as they drove away, "We'll be back to see you and your new home in a couple of months!"

Ryan asked, "Where are they going?"

Natty replied, "To the beach, maybe in Florida. Somewhere along the coast. They'll call and tell me."

Ryan noticed Tizzy and asked, "What do you have here?"

Tizzy followed Granddad and Nana to the car but was confused when they didn't pick her up to go.

Tizzy thought, "Wait, you forgot me! I'm not going for a car ride? You're leaving me! Oh, well! I get to stay here and play with my new friends! Yippee!"

Tizzy turned and ran to the pasture as the car drove out of sight. Tizzy played with Amber and Millicent Mink until she got tired.

Tizzy thought, "These critters are fun but I'm tired. I'll run to the porch and lay in the sun."

Megan sat down on the porch step and petted Tizzy.

Some of the other critters like Amber, Rona Rabbit, Millicent Mink, and Dallin Duck, noticed Tizzy on the porch and decided to join her.

Ryan followed everyone to the front porch and sat in one of the rocking chairs. Ryan said, "I came over to tell you that there's a party at the Mountain Lodge tomorrow night and to see if you're interested in going. It's a party for folks staying in the cabins so you're invited. I'll be there to help out, so you'll see my handsome face!"

Wendy laughed, then suggested to Allie, "Why don't we take Tizzy and go for a ride up to the Mountain Lodge and look around. We can get more information about tomorrow night. I want a map of the Valley."

"Ok, let's go!" Allie answered.

Wendy headed for the car while Allie got Tizzy and put her in the back seat. Once they arrived at the Lodge, Wendy said, "Let's let Tizzy follow us into the Lodge. Then we'll get an idea how much she strays from us."

As they entered the lobby, Tizzy spotted a man in a wheelchair holding a Pug. Tizzy ran over to them and jumped up.

The man said, "Well, well, would you look at that, Freddy! You have a friend here. What's her name?"

Allie said, "This is Tizzy. She's fairly new to our family but she's a real comedian!"

The man said, "Aren't they all! There's a lot going on here. They're planning a party for tomorrow night. Are you folks planning to come? Oh, here's my wife, Madeline. Madeline, come meet Tizzy, Freddy's new friend."

Wendy said, "Hi Madeline! Tizzy is a new member in our family. She's been with us a day! It looks like Tizzy has a mind of her own. I need to follow her. She went looking for something in the lobby. It was nice meeting you. Allie, I'll be right back."

Tizzy thought, "Freddy is a funny Pug, but I want to see what's outside."

Tizzy walked through the lobby to the long back wall of windows that reached from floor to ceiling. It was a great view of the flower garden outside.

Tizzy thought, "I want to go out to the pond."

Tizzy tried but couldn't find an opening to the outside. Tizzy pressed her nose against the window to get a good look. Then she turned and ran back to Freddy.

Wendy stopped by the front desk looking for information, then followed Tizzy, then went back to talk.

Allie told Wendy, "These folks are from Tennessee! Around Franklin. Wendy went to school in Nashville."

Wendy replied, "Small world. If you come to the party tomorrow, our family will be here, and you can meet them. We need to get back. Nice to meet you."

Tizzy led the way out the front door and back to the car. Once inside the car, Tizzy stood on the back seat looking outside as they drove back to the cabin.

Brody ran to Wendy's car as they drove up. He opened the back door to get Tizzy.

Brody said, "Come on Tizzy, let's have some fun." Brody took Tizzy over by the porch and put her down in the grass to watch.

Brody told Tizzy, "Sit and watch what I can do!"

Brody started doing cartwheels in the grass. Tizzy turned her head to the left and the right, trying to follow Brody's face as he went around in circles before her eyes. When that didn't work, Tizzy charged at Brody.

Megan said, "That was pretty funny! My turn with Tizzy. Come on, girl!"

Megan had a tote bag, the same green one that she used with Rona Rabbit at the Farmers Market. Megan laid the bag down and opened the top saying, "Come on Tizzy. Get in the bag!"

Tizzy climbed the three steps to the porch, sniffed at the bag, and crawled in.

Megan said, "Silly Tizzy, turn around!" as Megan tapped Tizzy to turn around.

Megan slowly picked up the bag carrying Tizzy. Just then Chris came out on the porch.

Chris said, "And what are you doing with Tizzy?"

Megan said, "Hal, Abbie Alpaca, and Darcy Pony stand too high to pay any attention to Tizzy. I want them to like Tizzy, so I thought that I'd lift Tizzy up to meet them. This seemed like an easy way to do it."

Chris called Brody, "Hey Brody! Do you feel like riding Darcy? Would you be interested in taking Tizzy for a ride with you?"

"Yeah, Dad! That's a great idea! Saddle up Darcy Pony! Give me Tizzy, Meg."

Megan said, "Don't grab her. Wait 'til you're on Darcy, then Dad can take her out of the tote bag and hand her to you."

Darcy Pony enjoyed giving Brody and Tizzy Pug a ride around the pasture, showing off to Hal and Abbie Alpaca. After several laps around the pasture, Darcy stopped to offload her passengers.

Brody opened the pasture fence gate and Tizzy started to run. She headed for the porch steps, turned, and ran around the cabin. On the back side of the cabin, Tizzy stopped by the bushes, and started to investigate. It didn't take long for Brody to catch up to her and try to grab her.

Tizzy was too quick. She finished her lap around the cabin, passed the front steps to the porch and headed toward the bottom of the hill toward the forest.

Brody was chasing Tizzy, yelling, "Stop, Tizzy!"

Tizzy kept running. She was determined to find something. Tizzy ran into the forest, and up the hill a short distance. Tizzy stopped and looked around.

Brody caught up with Tizzy and asked, "What is it?"

Tizzy moved a few steps and started digging.

"What are you doing, you crazy Pug! What do you think you are going to find? A pirate's treasure. Come on! Dad and Mom said that Megan and I were responsible for you. I'm hungry, so, you are coming with me. Now!"

Brody reached down and picked up Tizzy. Brody held on tight as Tizzy tried breaking loose.

Brody said, "Let's go back to the cabin. You're staying in the cabin tonight!"

Tizzy wrestled in Brody's arms and managed to jump to the ground.

Tizzy thought, "I don't want to be carried!"

Tizzy ran toward the porch. She was going to climb the steps to go into the cabin when the door opened. Todd and Megan came out.

Tizzy thought, "They aren't going to get me. I'm going to the pasture to play!"

Brody yelled, "Tizzy, get back here! Todd, you get her. I'm tired of wrestling with her."

Todd replied, "Just let her go, Brody. When she gets tired and hungry, she'll come back to the cabin."

Tizzy thought, "I'm going to play. There's Amber and Millicent Mink. I can play with them."

Millicent Mink saw Tizzy coming. Millicent rolled over and didn't move. She hoped that Tizzy would stand and stare at her, then go away. Millicent didn't expect Amber to poke her.

Amber thought, "Tizzy just wants to play!"

Tizzy thought, "They don't want to play. I can't do anything with Dallin Duck. Okay, I'll go back and see Brody. Maybe he'll take me for a walk around the cabin again."

Tizzy crawled under the fence rail and headed for the cabin. She climbed up the steps.

Tizzy thought, "I want Brody to walk with me."

Brody was sitting on the top step of the porch.

Tizzy jumped up on Brody to get his attention.

Brody said, "Come on Tizzy, one last walk around the cabin to explore. Then we're going into the cabin for dinner."

Tizzy ran down the steps and headed for the back of the cabin. Tizzy ran back to the same spot by the bushes and started to dig.

Brody yelled, "What are you looking for?"

Tizzy stopped digging just as Brody grabbed her and said, "Okay, this time you're not getting away. We're going inside!"

Mako and Stretch came running around the house and walked behind the bushes that Tizzy was inspecting.

Tizzy thought, "Put me down!"

Tizzy jumped out of Brody's arms and joined Mako and Stretch.

Todd yelled, "Brody! Come on, we're all waiting on you to eat!"

Tizzy turned and ran to the porch, looked up at Todd, then ran for the pasture.

Tizzy thought, "I want to play with that rabbit."

Todd said, "What's wrong, Brody. Can't you handle Tizzy?"

Brody made a face at Todd and exclaimed, "Yeah! You didn't see her! She keeps looking for something on the other side of the cabin. Look, even Mako and Stretch smelled something back there. I hope it isn't a hiding place for a skunk! Boy, we would have a mess trying to get Tizzy cleaned."

Todd said, "Just be glad there wasn't one to spray you! Come on in to eat and then watch a movie."

Brody yelled, "Okay, whose turn is it to pick one?"

Todd said, "Not yours!"

**<u>Interesting Information about the Pug</u>**

The Pug is a unique breed of dog that was brought from China to western Europe in the 1600s. The Pug eventually made its way to the United Kingdom by the 1900s. The Pug has features that are very different from other dogs. The Pug has a smooth and shiny coat, a lot of wrinkles, well-developed muscles, and has very short legs and body.

The Pug is an intelligent animal. It's a playful dog with a lot of energy and always ready to play a game. It acts like a clown, a watchdog, and a lover all rolled into one. The Pug is very smart, loving, loyal, and playful and especially loves children. It is a constant companion because it will follow you around wanting your attention and be with you everywhere you go, even to bed.

The Pug is also a good watchdog and doesn't tend to bark much. It is a quiet breed and not as active indoors as it is outdoors, making apartment living with a Pug a good choice. The Pug can be very determined to do what it wants when it wants making it stubborn at times. The Pug's stubborn nature can make training a Pug difficult. The Pug can be trained but you have to keep the Pug focused on listening to you.

### Tizzy Pug<sup>TM</sup>

In ***The Critter Family: Exploring the Shenandoah!***, Tizzy Pug<sup>TM</sup> is very young and playful and wants to be part of a family. Tizzy found the Critter Family at a perfect time to run and play with different critters in the pasture.

Tizzy Pug loves being around children. Tizzy especially liked to play with Brody and Megan. She went for walks with them and was able to roam and search without being controlled.

Tizzy Pug spent a lot of time around critters nearly her size like Amber and Millicent Mink. She liked them because they paid attention to her and played with her. Tizzy tried hard to make friends with everyone. She found that there were too many people and friends to choose from to follow. Tizzy needed to focus on who she wanted to follow around because she started getting under foot trying to get attention.

Tizzy has a strong sense of smell and loved finding things.

# Chapter 4 - The Finder

Everyone woke up to the early morning crowing from the neighbor's rooster. Allie and Todd went to the pasture to brush down Hal and Darcy Pony and to check on Abbie Alpaca. Wendy, Megan and Brody took Stretch and Mako  for a walk. After early morning chores were finished, everyone sat down for breakfast.

Chris said, "I'm going to Hank's after breakfast. If anyone wants to come along, I'm leaving in 10 minutes."

"Wow, I'm coming with you, Dad!" chimed Brody.

Ten minutes later, everyone was lined up at the truck, everyone except Natty.

Allie said, "Mom, Wendy and I will help you when we get back. We won't be gone long. But we've never been around an alpaca herd before!"

Natty said, "Okay, have fun. I'll be busy. I'll even take a walk with Tizzy and Amber. Can't imagine how that will work."

Wendy said, "Okay, I'll take my car since there's not enough room in the truck."

Megan and Brody immediately ran to Wendy's car.

After arriving at the alpaca ranch, Chris and Wendy went into the alpaca store to find Hank. Allie, Todd, Megan, and Brody wandered over to watch the alpaca herd and to talk to the alpacas.

Wendy shopped and took more alpaca items to her car. Wendy called over to the others, "Hank and Maggie are coming out in a few minutes to show us around the ranch. Does anyone else want to follow along?"

"YES!" they all yelled.

After a fascinating two-hour tour of the ranch, everyone headed back to the cabin. Natty waved as they drove up.

Natty said, "I've been busy scouting out the area for berry bushes and flowers. I spent a lot of time trying not to trip over Tizzy! She wants attention all the time and has so much energy. She followed me everywhere."

Wendy said, "Mom, wait 'til you see the alpaca things that I bought!" Wendy started opening her bags and to show off her new sweater and scarf.

Allie added, "We saw a lot of new things Maggie and Hank added to the store."

Wendy interrupted, "I don't mean to change the subject but who is that over there, Mom?"

Natty pointed to the side of the cabin and said, "While you were gone, I had company. Millicent Mink appears to have made a new friend. This little guy seems to like Millicent. He follows her around. This squirrel will be a friend to her, but he needs to learn not to scare her. We'll have to name him if he stays."

Natty continued to explain, "Millicent Mink's new friend is very active and is one of the few critters who comes out during the daytime. I watched him scurry around this morning looking for acorns, flower bulbs, even crackers that I threw to him. But Millicent is active at night. The two of them spend time playing early in the morning and then Millicent takes off to sleep or doing whatever she does. If this keeps up, I'll bet Tizzy will make friends with the squirrel."

The day went fast. Everyone was focused on going to the party that evening at the Mountain Lodge, so everyone was ready to eat dinner early.

Chris commented, "I think we should start making plans to go home. We need to name the squirrel, too! It's Wednesday. When should we head back?"

Wendy looked at her cellphone calendar and said, "I think we should go back on Saturday. That gives us time to do some hiking in the area and possibly get back over to the alpaca store and visit with Maggie."

Natty said, "All in favor, raise your hand!"

All hands went up except Brody's.

Brody replied, "I like it here. Why can't we go back Sunday? That gives us all day Saturday so that I can go to the festival Hank told us about."

Chris added, "Ok, we'll talk about it. Let's name the squirrel."

Natty said, "And Casey Cardinal's friend too!"

Allie added, "The squirrel is cute to watch. I think he should have a cute but simple name. He always scans the area for something to snatch and then hide."

Chris chimed in, "Let me name this one, I want a turn. He looks like a Scampy to me. Don't ask me why, but Scampy Squirrel$^{TM}$ seems right for him."

Natty laughed, then said "Ok, now we need to name Casey Cardinal's friend. Any suggestions?"

Wendy replied, "Since Casey's friend is dull in color and has streaks of red in the tail, I think it's a girl. I like the name Cara. Casey and Cara Cardinal$^{TM}$ sounds good – simple names."

Natty said, "Okay, Scampy and Cara it is!"

Todd commented, "Back to Scampy Squirrel. Scampy won't be interested in playing with the small, slower critters like Rona Rabbit or Dallin Duck. Scampy can run nearly half as fast as Hal, Mako and Stretch. If they run 40 miles per hour, Scampy can do about 15-20 miles per hour. I saw him run down the pasture fence. When he got near the corner, he would jump to the other fence rail which was at least 10 feet away. And if it was farther than that, his tail came out like a parachute in case he missed it. Scampy is the critter to watch, AND take pictures of, Wendy! He and Tizzy Pug should have fun together!"

While everyone was talking, Scampy Squirrel was searching under the hammock. He put something in his mouth and ran over to the cabin, dropping the object on the step. Scampy looked up at Megan who was standing in the doorway.

Megan said, "What do you have there, Scampy?" Megan stepped outside, picked up the object and said, "Look at this! Allie or Wendy, is this yours?"

Allie came out of the cabin, reached for her neck, and noticed that her necklace was missing. "Oh, when I laid in the hammock, I took my necklace off, because it kept falling around to my back. Then I fell asleep. It must have fallen to the ground. Scampy Squirrel found it! Thank you, little guy!"

Scampy Squirrel looked up with a cute look on his face and chirped, as though he understood Allie.

Todd went outside to watch.

Todd added, "Scampy Squirrel was digging all around the cabin! He's bringing things to the cabin steps. Scampy found a stash of marbles and a couple of Indian arrowheads. He even found this old coin!"

Chris opened the cabin door and went out on the porch.

Chris said, "Hmm, let me see that coin! My grandfather was a coin collector and taught me what to look for!"

Brody ran out of the cabin yelling, "Let me see! Hey, we still didn't finish talking about leaving Sunday!"

Chris said, "Ok, Brody. We'll finish talking about when to leave. Maybe when we go to the party tonight, we can find out more about the festival that Hank mentioned. Then we'll decide tomorrow."

Brody replied, "Okay, if I have to wait!"

Chris leaned over and picked up the old coin that Scampy found. Chris researched old items to learn where they came from and if there was any value. Chris's grandfather had a coin collection when Chris was young. Chris and his grandfather found several Indian arrowheads and a few old pennies that were made in the 1890s.

Brody said, "Look at Scampy Squirrel. He keeps bringing things. Where is he finding all this stuff?"

Just then, Scampy Squirrel stopped what he was doing and ran. He ran into the forest and up a tree.

Scampy thought, "What's that noise? Oh, this is a great view! I can see Abbie Alpaca, Darcy Pony, Hal, Mako, and Stretch playing in the pasture. But where is that noise coming from?"

Casey Cardinal and Cara Cardinal flew into the tree, resting on a branch near Scampy Squirrel. Without any warning, Scampy flipped an acorn scaring Casey and Cara. Casey and Cara flew off to land on the fence by Hal. Scampy thought, "I was trying to play. I guess birds scare easier than me!"

Scampy Squirrel thought, "I want to find that noise."

Scampy jumped from tree branch to tree branch in search of the quacking sound. He ran down the tree trunk and followed the sound into some bushes. Scampy found a duck stuck in a trap.

Scampy Squirrel thought, "I need help!" He ran down the hill to the pasture. Scampy ran in a circle around Chris and let out a shrill chirp.

Chris said, "What is it Scampy? Do you want me to follow you?" Scampy chirped hopping up and down.

Allie watched from the porch. She was sitting in a rocking chair talking on her cell phone when Scampy Squirrel ran to Dad. She watched as her Dad, Megan, Mako and Stretch ran from the fenced pasture area following Scampy Squirrel into the forest. Allie started running to catch up.

Chris yelled, "Mako, go help Scampy!"

Mako ran faster to keep up with Scampy.

Scampy Squirrel led everyone into the forest to a bush. Mako caught up with Scampy and found the duck. It was Dallin Duck!

By now, Chris, Megan, and Allie caught up with them by the bush.

Chris said, "Let's hurry! That quack is getting weak. Oh, no! It's Dallin Duck."

Allie said, "Dad, Megan can pull the bush apart while you get Dallin Duck loose. I'll reach in to pull him out."

Allie lifted Dallin Duck out of the bush and placed him on the ground.

Chris said, "I'm not sure what I'm looking at. I don't know if anything is broken. Megan, can you run to the cabin to get a large cloth tote bag to carry Dallin Duck in while I call Hank to find a veterinarian in the area?"

Chris phoned Hank.

Hank said "Just bring her over to my place. I'll look at her. Then we can call the veterinarian. He can decide if he needs to see Dallin Duck in his office."

Chris and Allie carefully placed Dallin Duck in the tote bag while Megan held it open.

Chris said, "Megan, you and Allie sit in the back seat and hold Dallin between the two of you while I drive to Hank's. Allie, call Mom to tell her where we are going. Tell Mom to go to the Mountain Lodge to the party and take Wendy, Todd, and Brody. Tell her to put Mako, Stretch and Amber in the cabin with Tizzy. We will join them when we are finished with Dallin."

Chris was relieved when they got to Hank's place. Chris noticed that Hank was gentle with animals.

Hank said, "Dallin Duck doesn't appear to have a broken leg or foot. It is swollen a lot."

Chris said, "Thank goodness because I don't know how to handle a duck with a broken leg!"

Hank called the veterinarian to get instructions. The veterinarian said, "Keep Dallin Duck still and put a bag of cold water with ice around his leg."

Hank got two plastic sandwich bags, filled them with cold water and ice, and put the bags in the tote bag.

Hank said to Chris, "Allie and I will hold the tote bag open while you lower Dallin Duck between the two ice bags."

Megan watched closely because she wanted to be a doctor when she grew up. She had a lot of questions.

Chris carried Dallin Duck to the car and drove back to the cabin.

Scampy Squirrel was waiting by the cabin steps when the truck pulled up.

Scampy Squirrel thought, "Dallin Duck sounds okay so I'm going to the pasture."

Chris and Allie carried the tote bag into the cabin.

Chris said, "Dallin Duck needs to spend the night in the cabin. Let's put him in the kitchen. Everyone, run and wash up and change your clothes. Let's go to the party."

Chris decided to put the critters up for the night. He ran back outside. He put Rona Rabbit and Millicent Mink in the horse trailer until he returned from the party. Then he turned on the flood lights to shine in the pasture. Just as the flood lights came on, the fox appeared outside the fence. The fox just sat there watching the field.

Scampy Squirrel thought, "I see eyes outside the fence. Who's out there? This is scary! I need to hide! If I run back and forth across the field in this zigzag pattern, I can get away from predators. I hope it's not going to chase me!"

Chris yelled to Scampy Squirrel, "Come here, Scampy! Don't be scared!"

Scampy ran over to Chris for help.

Chris said, "I'll put you in the horse trailer with Millicent Mink while we are at the party. Plan to sleep here tonight!"

Scampy thought, "I feel safe with my new critter friends. Thanks, Chris!"

Chris went back into the cabin and said, "Mako, you're in charge. Stretch, you help Mako. Dallin Duck will stay in the kitchen. Keep Tizzy away from Dallin and out of mischief. Amber will be alright in the house. Let me change my clothes. Then we can leave for the party!"

Chris ran upstairs to get ready. Ten minutes later he came downstairs.

Allie and Megan were waiting on the porch enjoying the country. Allie's phone rang.

Allie said, "It's Todd for you, Meg!"

Meg answered, "Hi, Todd. Okay, yes, I remember. Okay. Dad's upstairs changing. We'll be leaving soon. Okay, got it!"

Megan said, "I'll be right back. If Dad comes out, go to the truck. I'll meet you at the truck!"

Megan ran back into the cabin and was busy doing something for Todd.

Chris came out on the porch and said, "Where's Megan?"

Allie answered, "She needs to do something in the cabin. She said that she'll meet us in the truck. Is Scampy Squirrel alright? He seemed pretty scared."

Dad said, "Yes, he's in the horse trailer for the evening, maybe the night. I'm glad that we have a party to go to. We need a break! I'm looking forward to talking to folks about camping here in the Shenandoah."

Megan ran out from the cabin and jumped into the truck.

Megan said, "Okay, I'm ready!"

Dad continued saying, "I wonder if any of regular campers here fish much? I used to fish when I was growing up but I haven't fished for quite a while. I still have fishing rods but they're packed up back home. Maybe when we come back to visit Hank and Maggie, I can take you fishing and teach you how to bait a hook and cast a line. Would you be interested?"

Allie asked, "Yes, but do you need to wear those high boots to wade in the water or do you just stand on the bank?"

Megan said, "I do, Dad. I just don't want to touch the fish after I catch it. I bet Brody will touch my fish. I bet Brody will want you to teach him how to clean a fish. You can cut it open, but he would want to make a campfire and cook the fish over the campfire. Can we do that?"

Allie said, "Yes, but you need to get a bag of marshmallows. You can make S'mores!"

Megan laughed, "We better get mosquito spray while we're at it."

Allie said, "This is fun. I don't want to leave here. Now I'm anxious to come back. But I'll be back at school. You will get a chance to fish. If you come back, do you think that you'll stay in a cabin again, or where would you stay, Dad?"

Chris was pulling into the Mountain Lodge parking lot at that point and replied, "Wow, we haven't finished this vacation and you are already planning our next trip back here. Let's talk about this more tomorrow. When we meet Ryan inside, I'll talk to him about fishing in the area and places to stay for a few days when we come back. Now, let's go find your Mom!"

Megan said, "I can't wait to tell Todd and Brody about coming back to the Shenandoah to fish!"

**Interesting Information about the Squirrel**

The squirrel either lives and hangs in trees or it lives on the ground, digs in yards, and enjoys being around other squirrels by living in colonies. A tree squirrel likes to be alone. A tree squirrel can be one of 40 different types of tree squirrels that live in Europe, Asia, and the Americas. It is active in the daytime, makes a nest in holes in trees, and does not hibernate. It has excellent eyesight, even seeing in color. It can see behind its head because of the location of its eyes, just like rabbits. The squirrel that lives on the ground is very social and likes being around others. The squirrel is sneaky and likes to play tricks.

The squirrel isn't afraid of people but it is afraid of owls, hawks and cats which commonly attack them. The squirrel has different signals for alarms by using its voice and flipping its tail. It can make short, sharp sounds to a longer version of the sharp sound; or a moan that sounds like a whistle which is used for an air threat of a hawk. It has two tail signals. It either uses a twitch, or a wave of its tail or a flag signal like whipping its tail around in circles which is often used against a cat.

A squirrel eats things like seeds, nuts, tree cones, and fruits or it might eat meat like insects, small birds, young snakes, and small mice. A squirrel buries nuts so it's not available to eat and then it sprouts in the springtime. The squirrel only has a few food choices in the springtime - like buds on trees, cones, and bird seed! It especially appreciates food left outside, even birdseed.

The average lifespan of a squirrel is between 6-10 years. Most squirrels face daily threats and seldom live one year while squirrels living in a zoo can live over 20 years.

## Scampy Squirrel

In ***The Critter Family: Exploring the Shenandoah!***, Scampy Squirrel™ is a tree squirrel who is very active and loves to watch everything moving around him. He scans the area searching for things to snatch and hide. If he finds something that he can't eat, Scampy gives it to someone in the family. He finds lost things or interesting things lying around. Scampy likes to run and jump which made it possible to find Dallin Duck when Dallin needed help.

Scampy Squirrel started being a friend to Millicent Mink. Scampy quickly became a very loved and helpful member of the family.

# Chapter 5 - The Watcher

The party at the Mountain Lodge was crowded with a lot of talking, music, food, and drinks. There were quite a few regulars who stay in the cabins and know each other very well. Everyone was having fun and making friends.

Wendy walked over to Natty and said, "Mom, come meet the people that Allie and I met at the Lodge yesterday. The gentleman and his wife, Madeline have a Pug named Freddy."

Chris and Natty walked over and introduced themselves to Ed and Madeline.

Natty said, "I just spent the day alone with our Tizzy, and she is quite a character! I have a lot of questions about Pugs. When do they settle down and sleep?"

Ed laughed and said, "Maybe that's what I love the most about Freddy. He's willing to sit with me or to get up and run around. That entertains me because I'm tied up in this wheelchair for a while. I love watching him."

Chris said, "We would appreciate anything that you can tell us about what pugs are like. Tizzy has been with us a day and already we see how much energy she has."

Ed said, "They're fun but they have a mind of their own. They can be stubborn. They can be nosey. Don't ever think that you can ignore them or block them from entering a room. They'll find a way to squeeze through the smallest cracks to get anywhere they want."

Chris and Ed talked about pugs, camping, golf, and fishing for quite a while.

Chris laughed, then said, "Well, Ed, Madeline, it was so nice talking with you! I think we are going to head back to the cabin. We have a lot of critters to check on. Natty, I'm going over to the front desk to look for more information about the festival this weekend. Then I'll be ready to go."

When they arrived back at their cabin, the strangest sounds were coming from the living room.

Wendy said, "What is all that ruckus?"

Everyone climbed the steps to the cabin and were surprised the find Mako, Stretch, and Tizzy sitting in the living room in front of the television. Amber was sitting on the top of the couch.

Chris whispered, "What are they doing?"

Todd said, "Dad, what does it look like? They're watching a movie!"

Natty said, "How did this happen?"

Brody said, "Ryan helped us. Ryan showed us how to set up the video recorder and the TV to the pedal. We taught Mako how to step on this pedal to start the TV and the recorder."

Todd continued, "The DVD was already in the recorder. I called Megan. All she had to do before she left was to take Mako, Stretch, and Tizzy into the living room. Megan showed Mako how to start the movie. Then they sat back and watched."

Wendy said, "What are they watching?"

Brody said, "Oh, you know that movie about a dog that had an accident and met all his old friends. I don't think it was heaven because some of his friends were pretty bad. But maybe dogs have a dog heaven. I don't know. Anyways, they had fun watching it. Wait till we tell Ryan that it worked!"

Dad said, "Okay, I'm glad it worked! That was pretty creative. I'll have to ask Ryan about his other inventions. Todd, let's check that the critters are settled in the horse trailer for the night. Everything seems quiet around the cabin tonight."

Chris went to the front porch and whistled. Wendy came to the front porch asking, "What do you want?"

Chris said "Todd and I just checked on the critters in the horse trailer. Now we are going to walk around the pasture. Why don't you send Mako and Stretch out for one last run!"

Mako heard Chris and ran outside thinking, "I'm tired of Dallin Duck's quacking in the kitchen! Come on Stretch, let's run!"

Chris turned to Todd and said, "You get the fence lock while I grab the fish net. You're a young man and a big help to me! I can count on you, especially your good judgment handling these critters. Look, the fox is sitting by the fence watching the critters. I think it's time to talk to the fox again."

Chris and Todd walked toward the fox. The fox started to back up into the tree area.

Chris said, "Hey, Mr. Fox. I just want to talk to you. What are you watching when you sit here?"

The fox recognized Chris's voice and sat back down.

Chris said "I know that you like to hunt at night, but you're also out during the daytime. You don't have to be afraid of me. I won't hurt you. If you want to join this critter family, you'll need to get along with all of them.

You can't scare any of them, or my family. Do you want to meet some of the critters?" Chris watched for the fox's reaction, then turned to walk toward the fence gate.

The fox sat there and watched them walk away.

Chris called to the fox, "Come on! I'll let you in the pasture." On the way through the gate, Chris grabbed the rope that hung on the fence. The fishing net and the rope were put there in case of an emergency.

Mako, Stretch, Abbie Alpaca, and Darcy Pony walked over to Chris. Hal stayed along the back fence. The critters seemed to sense that the fox was friendly.

Mako thought, "This guy seems okay. What do you think, Stretch? Let's run with him and see if he's scary?

Mako and Stretch started to walk around as if they were playing, then they slowly ran towards Hal.

Mako barked at the fox saying, "Come run with us!"

Chris said to the fox, "Go on!"

Todd said, "Dad, the fox seems friendly, but we don't know what he's really like yet."

A short time later, Chris yelled, "Mako, Stretch, time to go in."

Chris told Todd, "I'll try to get the fox to follow us and see if he'll spend the night in a cage in the back of the truck. I'll keep the cage door unlocked."

Mako and Stretch charged toward the cabin.

Natty opened the door to let them in.

The fox slowly followed Chris and Todd to the truck.

Chris said to the fox, "You can spend the night in the truck or you can go back up the mountain. If you want to join the critter family, you need to decide quickly. We are leaving in a few days to go home. You can either stay in the truck tonight or go back up the mountain."

The fox slowly turned away from Chris and started walking away toward the trees.

The fox looked back at Chris and thought, "I want to stay, but the easiest thing for me to do is to roam during the night. I don't want to scare anyone, but I'm not ready to join the critters tonight. Maybe I could watch Hal, Abbie Alpaca, and Darcy Pony in the field for a while longer."

The fox turned and walked away.

Chris and Todd went into the cabin.

Chris said to Natty, "The fox seems friendly enough. I told the fox that if he wants to join the critter family, he has to get along with all of them."

Natty replied, "Really, Chris, of all our critters, Millicent Mink is the only one that I'm cautious around. Now you're talking about a fox joining the critter family! The fox might turn on Dallin Duck, Rona Rabbit, or Millicent Mink. Don't forget that we have Tizzy! We need to do a lot of talking to the fox over the next few days so that he trusts us and is friendly."

Allie said "I don't know about this. You better be careful because I won't be here to help you. I'm concerned about Hal."

Todd replied, "I'll be watching Hal. Dad and I watched the fox, and he seems to want a home. We still have two more days or maybe three if we stay for the festival."

Early the next morning, the fox came to the cabin door making chirping sounds.

Chris said, "Natty, what's that sound?"

Chris went outside and sat on the step.

The fox sat next to Chris. The fox pushed Chris's hand with his nose. The fox laid his head down on his paws. Chris reached out and patted the fox's head.

The fox thought, "I'm tired of roaming the mountain. I want new friends. I don't want you to be afraid of me."

Chris called out, "Todd, would you bring out some food for the fox. He seems to want to stay."

Todd came back to the porch and said, "I looked up 'food for a fox' on the computer. A fox eats almost anything. Here's a dish with an egg, berries, and chicken."

Chris got up to lead the fox over to the truck.

Chris said to the fox, "You'll sleep here if you stay with us."

The fox gave a chirp as if to say "Yes", then turned and ran toward the pasture.

Natty walked over to the truck and said to Chris, "We have to name the fox."

Todd said, "I've been thinking about that, and I have a name! What do you think of Fifer Fox$^{TM}$?"

Natty said, "Whatever the name is, I want him to get used to his name before we go home."

Chris walked to the fenced pasture and called the fox. "Welcome to the critter family! We decided to call you Fifer Fox!"

The fox chirped and leaped in the air.

"Okay Fifer Fox, Mako and Stretch are waiting to run with you."

Fifer Fox turned and ran to catch Mako and Stretch.

Chris told Natty, "Before all the critters pile into the truck or horse trailer, they're going to get cleaned up."

Chris yelled, "Wendy, Allie, Todd, come help me?"

Wendy came out of the cabin, and Allie came in from the fenced pasture area.

Todd said, "What do you want, Dad?"

Chris asked, "Can you help me set up a small tub and a hose to wash the critters before we go home?"

Allie said, "Are you kidding me? How can I find a small tub here?"

Chris said, "Call Hank. Maybe they have something that we can use. Natty, bring Tizzy out. She can watch and get more acquainted with the other critters."

Allie, Wendy, and Todd jumped into the truck to drive to Hank's ranch. They came back quickly with a tub and soap to clean the critters.

Todd and Brody lined up the critters.

Allie said, "We can shower Hal first. He is the largest, and all the other critters can watch and see how easy it is. If Hal can do it, they can do it."

Todd said, "I'll help you, Allie! Hal loves being groomed. What's a little more water?"

Allie replied, "Tell that to Hal! We'll see how much water Hal really likes!"

Some of the critters started moving around as if they wanted to run away. Tizzy was annoying the critters by walking between them, then standing up on her back legs to get attention.

Hal was sprayed with water, and he whinnied to tell the critters, "This feels good! The water isn't cold!"

Chris yelled, "Who's next?"

Tizzy ran to Chris and thought, "I want to be sprayed too! It looks like fun."

Megan grabbed Tizzy to get her out of the way. Stretch thought, "This is fun!" Mako took one step forward. As Chris scrubbed Mako, Stretch and Fifer Fox jumped into the tub splashing water all over.

Wendy laughed and said, "Okay, you're getting it!"

Chris sprayed Stretch and Fifer Fox with the hose, and Wendy added the soap.

Fifer Fox jumped out of the tub thinking, "Stretch, you're crazy!"

The critters had fun. Rona Rabbit jumped and did a binky. Mako shook off the bath water and ran to the pasture to join Hal. Stretch took longer getting washed.

Allie thought, "This is a great time to take pictures."

Chris called out, "Who's next?" The critters took turns starting with Dallin Duck, then Millicent Mink, then Abbie Alpaca, then Darcy Pony, then Scampy Squirrel.

Casey Cardinal and Cara Cardinal wanted no part of it and flew away.

Fifer Fox was last, moving slowly and thinking, "I only get wet when I cross a river. What is soap?"

Fifer was still wet and covered with soap. He kept watching Mako and Stretch running in the field.

Fifer thought, "Okay, I don't like this but hurry up and finish!"

Chris said, "That wasn't so bad, Fifer. Go join Mako and Stretch."

Fifer Fox ran to join Mako and Stretch.

Ryan drove up to pick up the tub that Allie borrowed. He walked to the pasture and stood by the fence to watch the critters, but he couldn't ignore Tizzy.

Tizzy thought, "I want you to pick me up!"

Ryan picked her up and yelled to Chris, "I don't know what you feed this bunch, but they're happy and having fun running around."

Chris yelled, "Come sit on the porch."

Ryan yelled, "Abbie, Darcy, come with me!"

Ryan led Abbie and Darcy to the front porch.

Ryan said, "Abbie, sit down!"

Abbie climbed the steps to the porch and sat at the top of the stairs. Darcy walked around the porch searching for something to do.

Brody came out of the cabin and said, "Oh, neat! Come here Darcy. I'm going to ride you bareback!"

Ryan said, "That will give Darcy something to do!"

Chris said, "Do you do a lot of work with electronics? We saw your television and video recorder contraption! I'm curious to know what else you've created! Tell me about yourself, Ryan."

Ryan said, "I don't live here in the Shenandoah, Chris. I was raised here but moved away for college and work. I just arrived a few days before you came to the cabin. I'm spending a month here to help my folks."

Chris said, "We were surprised last night to find Mako, Stretch, and Tizzy watching a movie. They apparently started it after we left using your device. I'd be interested in hearing about other things you've created."

Ryan replied, "Well, Chris, that's a long story, but I do have some pictures with me that I can show you. I spent two years at a technology institute before I transferred to a college for an engineering degree."

Chris said, "Now you have my attention. We have a lot to talk about, and it's not about critters! Wendy has an engineering degree, and Allie is completing hers! We can have some good conversations later."

### Interesting Information about the Fox

The fox is nearly everywhere in the world except Antarctica. The fox usually avoids humans and doesn't usually attack humans.

The fox is related to wolves and dogs and has common characteristics to a cat. A male fox is called a dog fox and a female fox is called a vixen. Grey fox that live in North America are the only type of dog fox that climbs trees. It can run between 30 to 40 miles per hour and can jump at least six feet high.

The fox lives in a small family but is alone most of the time to hunt and sleep. A fox lives in a den, usually with three or four vixen fox and dog fox. The fox eats things like berries, worms, spiders, and small animals like mice and birds. If it lives in the city, it will eat garbage that people leave out.

The fox's whiskers on its face and legs help it to navigate. The pupils of its eyes are vertical, like a cat's eyes, which helps the fox to see better at night. The fox has excellent hearing. It has an odor or smell that comes from scent glands at the base of its tail. The fox has a beautiful coat of fur.

The fox is a very playful critter that loves playing with balls. It makes about 40 different sounds but its scream is pretty scary.

The fox average lifespan is from one to three years. A few could live as long as 10 years.

**Fifer Fox**
In ***The Critter Family: Exploring the Shenandoah!*,**

Fifer Fox is a very careful and watchful critter who stayed away from people. He was a loner but is tired of roaming the mountains and now is looking for friends. Fifer is spotted repeatedly watching the critters in the fenced pasture in the Shenandoah Valley during the day and night. He wanted to make friends with the critters after watching how much fun they had together. Fifer sat outside the fence at night watching the critters in the pasture but it scared Abbie Alpaca. He was chased up the mountain by Darcy Pony because he scared Abbie. Fifer soon was invited to be part of the critter family and quickly became running friends with Mako and Stretch.

# Chapter 6 - The Lockpicker

Everyone woke up early the next morning. Instead of getting ready to drive home, Brody convinced them to stay longer to go to the local festival!

Megan said, "This festival sounds like fun! It's a combo festival."

Todd asked, "What's a combo festival?"

Allie answered, "Well, there are different kinds of festivals. There are music festivals, food festivals, craft festivals, or wine festivals. This one is advertised to be a little of all four."

Brody said, "What kind of food will they have? I think drinking wine is dumb. It's easier to just eat the grapes!"

Natty laughed, "It takes a lot of work and time to make wine. Let's stick with foods that we usually don't have! Let's plan to eat brunch there. Thanks for insisting on going to the festival. That was a good idea, Brody!"

The festival was crowded. Natty and Megan wanted to find Hank and Maggie's stand. Chris took Todd and Brody to search for tasty foods while Wendy and Allie went to the music pit.

Everyone met up after an hour to share their favorite spots. By this time, everyone was hungry.

Todd said, "We found a good place to eat. It has a several things but I want to try tapas."

Natty replied, "Let's go! I like trying foods that I haven't cooked."

Megan asked, "Where do they make tapas, I mean which country?"

Todd replied, "Spain, their sign mentioned Spain."

It was a long day of walking, eating, and talking to Hank, Maggie, and Ryan. Everyone was tired and wanted to go back to the cabin. It was time to call it a day.

Chris drove up to the cabin and exclaimed, "Oh, no! Who left the gate open? Abbie Alpaca is sitting on the porch with Fifer Fox. Let's check the horse trailer and the pasture. Count the critters and let's see if they're all here."

None of the critters were missing. They just weren't where they were supposed to be.

Natty said, "Okay everyone. Let's get a good night's rest. We have a busy day tomorrow, especially after we get back home!"

Chris woke up early the next morning to pack everything up for the trip home. Allie and Todd were busy feeding all the critters.

Wendy said, "Allie and Todd can ride with me in the SUV. We will take Mako, Stretch, Amber, Rona Rabbit, and Dallin Duck. You get the rest, Dad! Oh, we can handle Tizzy Pug!"

Chris said, "Well, the horse trailer will carry Hal, Abbie Alpaca, Darcy Pony, and Millicent Mink. The bed of the truck can carry Fifer Fox in a cage, Casey Cardinal and Cara Cardinal in a cage, and Scampy Squirrel in a cage."

Natty asked Allie, "Can you and Brody please check the pasture to make sure that nothing is left in the field?"

Chris added, "I'll make one last check in the cabin to make sure that nothing was left in drawers or under beds or in closets."

Natty sighed saying, "And I will walk around the outside of the cabin to check for anything left outside."

Brody yelled, "I'll help you, Mom. I'll bring Tizzy for one last run around the cabin."

Brody and Tizzy ran around the cabin. Tizzy started to bark when she got to the backside of the cabin.

Brody said, "That's strange! Tizzy stopped at the same spot a few days ago. She smells something."

Natty pulled back the bushes and discovered a little raccoon. The raccoon was all alone. It looked up at Natty with sad eyes.

Natty asked Brody, "Would you run and get a carton of milk out of the cooler? I'll keep Tizzy here with me."

Brody ran back to the truck, poured milk into a lid, and brought it back to the raccoon.

Chris walked around the cabin to see what was going on.

Natty said, "Chris, we can't leave this little raccoon here. Can you and Todd walk around, maybe over by the forest, to see if you can find a raccoon family? We can't leave it here all by itself!"

Chris sighed and said, "We were just about to get the critters settled in the horse trailer and SUV for the trip. Alright, Todd and I will go search for a raccoon family!"

Chris called Todd, "Hey Todd, give me a hand."

Chris and Todd walked toward the base of the mountain. Fifer Fox ran past them.

Chris yelled, "Fifer, get back here!"

But it was too late. Fifer Fox ran into the trees and out of sight.

Todd said, "Now what, Dad? How will we find Fifer Fox?"

Chris replied, "One critter at a time. Let's see if we can find a raccoon family. Let's spread out along the base of the mountain and hope we find some raccoons quickly, then we can look for Fifer Fox."

Chris stopped, looked over at the cabin and saw Tizzy running toward the forest. Brody was chasing her.

Chris exclaimed, "What is going on? We're going home in a few minutes, and we've lost control of the critters. How long is it going to take us to round up those rascals?"

A few minutes later, Chris yelled to Natty, "Find another cage! There isn't a raccoon family anywhere near here."

Tizzy ran into the forest and found Scampy Squirrel there. Tizzy started running in circles around Scampy.

Scampy Squirrel thought, "I found a box but I can't dig it out. I need help! This is too much work for me. Tizzy, stop jumping around and dig!"

Brody caught up with Tizzy and said, "Scampy, what are you doing here? You're supposed to be in the truck! Wait 'til Dad finds out. Look at you. You're digging in the same spot that Tizzy was digging the other day. Only this time, you found something! It's a box that's bigger than you! Wow! Maybe it's a pirate's treasure! I'll help, but first, I have to take Tizzy back to the car."

Brody grabbed Tizzy and headed out of the forest to put Tizzy in Wendy's car.

Brody said to Tizzy, "If Dad sees you, you're in trouble! You're covered with dirt. I need to find a brush or towel to wipe you off. Wendy won't want you in her car like this!"

Meanwhile, Scampy Squirrel was in the forest and started jumping up and down and chirping to send out an alert call.

Fifer Fox heard Scampy Squirrel and was on his way to find Scampy in the forest. Fifer reached Scampy and found him digging up a big box.

Scampy Squirrel chirped saying, "Help me dig!"

Fifer Fox replied, "Move over Scampy, the dirt is going to fly!"

Mako barked, "Hey Stretch, come with me."

Mako and Stretch ran into the forest and found Scampy and Fifer throwing dirt all over.

Mako thought, "They're not going to get that box out!"

Mako barked, "Fifer Fox! Get that rope hanging on the fence."

Fifer Fox chirped, "Okay!"

Fifer Fox ran to the pasture fence and pulled on the rope. The rope was stuck on the fence. Fifer grabbed the rope with his teeth and jumped high in the air but the rope didn't come off the fence. Fifer fell to the ground, holding the end of the rope in his teeth.

Fifer Fox rested for a minute, then thought, "I need that rope. This time, I'll jump and then grab the rope."

Fifer Fox jumped as high as he could, then grabbed the rope in his teeth. Fifer's head jerked forward as he fell to the ground.

Fifer Fox laid on the ground thinking, "My teeth hurt! Now, what do I do? Mako is waiting for me to bring the rope. I have an idea!"

Fifer Fox ran to the horse trailer and chirped to Darcy Pony, "Darcy, I need your help! Follow me!"

Darcy Pony climbed out of the trailer and followed Fifer Fox over to the pasture fence.

Fifer Fox chirped, "I need that rope. Can you get it off the fence? I need to take it to Mako in the forest."

Darcy Pony whinnied, "I got it, Fifer Fox. Stand back!"

Darcy reached up, grabbed the rope and pulled it up over the fence post.

Darcy whinnied, "Here, Fifer."

Fifer Fox chirped, "Thanks, Darcy Pony! Now follow me! We need to help Scampy Squirrel!"

Brody was standing by the car and handed Tizzy to Wendy. Brody saw Darcy Pony running away.

Brody yelled, "Darcy Pony, where are you going? Mom, some of the critters are running away! I'm going to follow them!"

Fifer Fox and Darcy Pony reached the others in the forest. Fifer chirped, "Here's the rope, Mako."

Mako grabbed the rope and dropped it over the box. Mako barked, "Scampy, put the rope around the box."

Then Mako barked at Darcy Pony, "Pull the rope and drag the box out of the hole, Darcy. Ready, go!"

The box came out of the hole. The critters made a good team! Scampy Squirrel ran out of the forest as if he was leading everyone back to the cabin. Darcy Pony was pulling the box with Mako and Fifer Fox following her and barking. Stretch ran to meet Brody and decided it was time to do a zoomie to let off some steam!

Brody yelled, "Megan, come and look what they found! Todd, come quick. They need help with the box! It might be a pirates treasure hidden in the woods!"

Todd ran over to meet Brody.

Todd said, "Brody, I'll help Darcy Pony and carry this box to the cabin. You can help me."

Todd grabbed the rope from Darcy and lifted the box with Brody's help.

Todd said, "This is heavy! I wonder what's in it!"

Brody said. "Maybe some hidden gemstones or pirates' treasure!"

Todd scoffed, "Pirates in the Shenandoah! Wow, maybe Davey Crockett stuff!"

Everyone gathered in front of the cabin to check out the treasure box. Ryan drove up and got out of his truck.

Ryan said, "Allie called me. She said that some of the critters aren't ready to go home yet! I brought the tub and soap back over to set up a shower again."

Chris replied, "We were ready two hours ago, then Natty found a raccoon, and the critters ran all over the place!"

Todd laughed and said, "Mom found a baby raccoon. Dad and I searched for a raccoon family in the area and noticed Fifer Fox running into the woods. Scampy Squirrel uncovered a treasure box. Now we are looking for another cage to take this baby raccoon home with us."

Chris replied, "Now we know why Fifer Fox was running into the forest! You started it Scampy Squirrel!"

Turning to the critters, Chris said, "Line up! You know if you need a shower. The first one to shower is the one who started all this in the forest."

A little chirp came from the back of the group. The critters moved to let it pass. It was Scampy Squirrel jumping up and down chirping, "Look at my box!"

Wendy said, "Tizzy is in my car. I wiped the dirt off her. Allie and I will shower them, Dad. You start loading the other critters into the vehicles."

Scampy Squirrel jumped in the tub. He wanted to hurry getting his shower so that he could guard his box!

Fifer Fox and Mako were the last ones needing a shower. When they finished, they started running around the cabin.

Stretch thought, "I don't need a shower. I didn't work hard!"

Natty stood there watching the critters. She quietly walked over to Scampy Squirrel's box.

"What do you have there, Scampy," Natty said as she tried to open the latch.

Natty continued, "Chris, this is really interesting. If the box was in the forest, then it wasn't on this property. The box is locked so it may not be easy to find the owner. Do you think we should call your friend who owns the cabin to ask if he buried anything in the mountain side?"

Chris said, "Yes, I'll call him and see what I can find out. But right now, let's get the rest of these critters in place for the trip home. Ryan, thanks again for coming to our rescue! You made our trip home more pleasant!"

Natty said goodbye to Ryan. "Come visit us!"

Natty turned toward the truck and said, "Chris, I decided to put the small cage between our seats in the front of the truck so that the little raccoon could see us."

Chris said, "Okay, Todd and I need to finish getting the critters in place for the trip."

Chris turned to get the critters just as Mako and Stretch ran past the truck, past the cabin, and out of sight.

Chris yelled, "Mako, Stretch, get back here!"

Chris told Todd, "There better be a good reason for this! Let's go!"

Chris and Todd ran past the cabin to see what was going on. They were amazed at the sight. Fifer Fox was leading a herd of deer down the road from the Mountain Lodge. Mako and Stretch ran to join the herd.

Todd yelled back to the vehicles, "Hey everyone, come here! You have to see this!"

Wendy and Allie jumped out of the SUV. Megan and Brody ran to catch up with Dad and Todd.

Dad said, "Don't even think about it! None of those deer are coming back with us! I don't know what Fifer Fox thought he was doing, but Fifer can say his goodbyes now or he can stay here!"

Natty laughed saying, "Relax, Chris. Fifer Fox probably told his friends that he was moving away. They are coming to say goodbye and send him off."

Natty turned to the kids and said, "Focus on putting the critters into the vehicles. We need to do it quickly or another one will run off. I'm certain that we'll bring Fifer back here when we visit Hank. Fifer would be excited to go back to the Mountain Lodge and visit his friends!"

Fifer Fox walked to the truck, turned around, and leapt into the air giving off a loud chirp! The deer herd made a ruckus and nodded their heads saying goodbye. Fifer was happy. He jumped into the truck bed to leave with his new family!

After the critters were in the horse trailer and SUV, Chris and Todd jumped into the vehicles, exhausted.

Natty said, "Megan and Brody, buckle up. You can watch the raccoon at home."

It was a quiet trip home because everyone was tired!

Chris drove up their driveway at Dunn Stable and saw someone walking away from their front door. It was Paul, their neighbor.

Pau7l said, "Hi, I have good news and bad news, Chris. I wanted you to be the first to know that we are moving."

Chris joked saying, "Is that the good news or the bad news?"

Paul laughed.

Chris asked, "A transfer?"

Paul said, "We are buying a home in Atlanta for Lori to be near family. I'm taking a job in Nashville for two years, then I'll join her. It's only a four-hour drive from Nashville to Atlanta so I'll travel there on weekends."

Chris said, "That's great!"

Paul continued, "Lori is planning to grow a large flower garden in Atlanta. She wants to see how much business she'll have selling flowers. Her garden should grow a lot faster there. The growing season is longer, and it is more humid in Atlanta."

Natty said, "We'll miss you, but we wish you well!"

Paul hesitated, then said, "We haven't decided what to do with our parrots yet since we just got them. Your critter family has grown since you went to the Shenandoah. Would you consider adding parrots?"

Natty said, "We can talk it over tonight. How hard can two parrots be!"

Paul added, "Hey, I see you had a flagpole installed while you were away. That is a nice-looking flagpole. It will be great to see 'Old Glory' flying in the neighborhood."

Chris replied, "If you need any help moving, just call us. Just don't call today – I'm tired!"

Everyone started to unload the critters, putting Hal, Abbie Alpaca, Darcy Pony, Mako, and Stretch into the pasture. Dallin Duck, Millicent Mink and Scampy Squirrel went to the pond. Fifer Fox laid on the front porch.

Natty told Chris, "Let Casey and Cara Cardinals out to fly! I'm not sure where to put the raccoon. Raccoons are night critters, just like Fifer Fox and Millicent Mink. I can put his cage under the tree not far from Rona Rabbit's old rabbit hole. He'll be out of the way there. Rona and Amber are on the back patio playing. Tizzy goes in the house. She's a handful right now."

Natty, Wendy, and Allie got busy preparing dinner and set it out on the patio.

Chris rang the dinner bell, and all the critters came. The raccoon sat watching them.

Natty opened the cage for the raccoon to join the critters. Natty said, "We have to give this little fellow a name. Any suggestions?"

Wendy said, "This one is mine, I like Roxbury Raccoon™."

Brody said, "Roxbury! Who names a raccoon Roxbury?"

Allie said, "Brody, you can name another critter. It's Wendy's turn. I actually like Roxbury, it makes him sound clever! Roxbury Raccoon may be little, but he is clever. It's a waste of time to put Roxbury in a cage, he figured out how to unlock the latch. When he gets out, he doesn't go far from the back patio. Rona Rabbit and Amber seemed to be watching out for Roxbury."

Several days passed. Wendy was having second thoughts about leaving Mako and Amber behind. Wendy raised Mako, and he was her loyal buddy. Now Mako and Amber would be staying with Mom and Dad for a while longer. But Wendy needed to make plans to drive home, so she focused on what she wanted to do before leaving. Her plans included giving Mako and Stretch more obedience training.

Wendy sighed thinking, "I need to get home, but I am going to miss the family and all the critters!"

Allie was putting in a lot of time riding Hal before she returned to college.

The critters were getting to know each other better. Tizzy was having fun in the critter family. The night critters like Millicent Mink, Fifer Fox, and Roxbury Raccoon spent part of their time in the morning with everyone before they rested during the day.

Scampy Squirrel stayed after dinner, playing with Roxbury Raccoon. Scampy started teaching Roxbury how to climb trees. The two of them played in the trees in the back yard, sitting on a large tree branch watching Hal and the others in the pasture. Millicent Mink joined them.

The Cardinals would land on branches chirping which gave Chris an idea.

Chris thought, "I'm going to surprise the tree critters. I'll build a tree house for them to play and sleep in."

Chris asked Todd, "Would you like to help me with another building project?"

Todd said, "What is it this time, Dad?"

Dad said, "I wanted it to be a surprise, but that's hard. It's a tree house! I bought all the materials that we need to build it. We can get started."

Chris and Todd got to work. Tizzy followed them back and forth from the stable to the tree to watch them work. Chris and Todd completed the tree house in three days including long winding stairs that spiraled down to the ground.

Allie said, "Megan and I will paint it. It will be different colors so that it will be easy to see."

Millicent Mink quickly found the tree house. Millicent climbed the stairs and stayed up in the trees for hours with Scampy Squirrel and Roxbury Raccoon. Fifer Fox climbed the stairs and watched Mako and Stretch run in the pasture with Hal, Abbie Alpaca, and Darcy Pony.

Natty said to Chris, "We have to figure out what to do with Tizzy. She wants to follow Scampy Squirrel up to the tree house."

Roxbury Raccoon was getting bigger now and started roaming from the house. He would roam at night with Millicent Mink and Fifer Fox. The three of them were creating mischief in the neighborhood, primarily the night before trash pickup.

Chris was tired of hearing the neighbors complain about the trash mess so he told Todd his plan.

Chris said, "I have those three critters figured out. We're going to close the stable doors and lock the mischievous critters in the stable twice a week - the night

before the trash truck is scheduled to pick up trash! I'll need your help, Todd."

Todd agreed, "I'll remind you, Dad! Those three are sneaky and messy!"

Fifer Fox, Millicent Mink and Roxbury Raccoon liked roaming at night and resting during the daytime. Fifer usually slept at the base of the tree in the bushes with Millicent, while Scampy Squirrel and Roxbury were up in the tree house.

One afternoon, Chris said to Natty, "I am going to test Roxbury Raccoon's dexterity with his hands. I'll put treats in 13 boxes. We'll see if Roxbury will use things like hooks, bolts, buttons, latches, and levers to get to the treats. Some boxes will have more than one lock. Let's see how he does!"

Roxbury thought, "This looks like fun!" and quickly started working on the locks.

Chris said, "Wow! Roxbury opened 11 of them. I need to research raccoons. I know that raccoons are great problem solvers and learn quickly to figure things out, but I didn't think that they were that good. I'm going to put three different types of locks on the tree house so that Roxbury can unlock them every day."

After dinner on the patio, Chris said, "I think that we should offer to take the parrots. The parrots would help us keep an eye on the other critters. They are smart, and the critters would have fun listening to parrots. What do you think? Should we tell Paul and Lori yes?"

Natty smiled and quickly said, "Yes, talking birds will amuse the other critters. Let's go tell them!"

Chris and Natty walked down the street to tell Paul. The packers arrived that day and packed boxes were everywhere. The parrots were in their cages on the back deck far away from the packing noise.

Chris said to Paul, "We will adopt the parrots. Just let us know when you want us to take them."

Lori said, "Oh, thank you! We know they'll be happy with you. Besides, look at the critter family they'll be joining!"

Natty replied, "Yes, look at them! Can you even imagine that we are planning to take them on a trip to Wyoming in a few weeks?"

**Interesting Information about the Raccoon**

 The Raccoon is native to most of North America and can be found in parts of Europe and Japan. It is a mammal and has gray fur with a black mask, and seven black rings around its tail. The raccoon is active at night (nocturnal) and hibernates in its den in the wintertime. It is mostly found in heavily wooded areas near trees, vegetation, and water. It usually makes its home in attics, sewers, sheds, and barns. The raccoon is also a great climber making it easy to get shelter and food.

The raccoon has front paws with very flexible toes. A raccoon can easily use its toes to grab things. It can use its toes to open doors, latches, and bottles because its toes are flexible giving it an amazing skill (dexterity).

The raccoon eats vegetation like fruit, and meat like frogs, worms, and fish. It cleans its food before eating it by rinsing it with water or rubbing it to remove dirt. It will travel miles in search of food. The raccoon will tip over garbage cans, destroy gardens, and even damage property if food is hard to find. It has a reputation of being a nuisance because it damages property.

The raccoon likes living where people live but can be very unfriendly, even vicious, if it is approached. It uses over 200 different sounds and about 12 different calls to communicate. The raccoon is a very intelligent and curious critter, living in small groups of 4-5 critters called a nursery. It wants protection from predators like dogs and coyotes. The raccoon preys on rabbits, snakes, frogs, lizards, and nesting birds.

The raccoon becomes a hazard when it is carrying roundworms or rabies which would make a raccoon act mean or very aggressive, make strange sounds, or foam from the mouth. The local animal control authority should be called quickly if a raccoon is spotted with one of these problems. Raccoons ARE NOT recommended as pets.

The raccoon has an average lifespan living in the wild of two to three years but up to 20 years in captivity.

**Roxbury Raccoon**
In ***The Critter Family: Exploring the Shenandoah!***,
 Roxbury Raccoon™ was very small when he was discovered so he learned how to be around different critters very early. Roxbury was not the average raccoon. Roxbury is not a loner and has fun around people. Roxbury quickly makes friends with Rona Rabbit and Amber. He immediately begins using his skillful fingers to unlock locks. Roxbury is mischievous when he roams the neighborhood at night.

# References

1. ALPACA:
https://en.wikipedia.org/wiki/Alpaca
https://www.mnn.com/earth-matters/animals/stories/10-things-you-didnt-know-about-alpacas
https://www.livescience.com/52668-alpacas.html
https://alpacameadows.com/the-alpacas/the-facts-about-alpacas/
2. SHETLAND PONY:
https://en.wikipedia.org/wiki/Shetland_pony
https://www.petguide.com/breeds/horse/shetland-pony/
3. PUG:
https://en.wikipedia.org/wiki/Pug
https://dogtime.com/dog-breeds/pug#/slide/1
https://petcentral.chewy.com/dog-breeds-pug/
http://www.petpugdog.com/pug-dog-behavior-temperament
4. SQUIRREL:
https://en.wikipedia.org/wiki/Squirrel
https://www.livescience.com/28182-squirrels.html
5. FOX:
https://en.wikipedia.org/wiki/Fox
https://www.mentalfloss.com/article/59739/14-fascinating-facts-about-foxes
https://animalinyou.com/animals/fox/
6. RACCOON:
https://en.wikipedia.org/wiki/Raccoon
https://animals.mom.me/characteristics-of-raccoons-5040993.html

# A Request by the Author

Thank you for your continued following of The Critter Family.

Follow me for the latest tales of The Critter Family by visiting my *website* at
https://www.barbarabanks.studio/home
or https://www.instagram.com/barbarabanks.author
or https://www.facebook.com/barbarabanks.author

# About the Illustrator

Virginia based illustrator, Rossnelly Salazar, creates artwork ranging from kidlit whimsy and humor to young adult, each embedded with a story to tell.

Rossnelly is a graduate from the Maryland Institute College of Art, having earned her BFA and MA in Illustration, where she practiced illustration, book illustration, animation, concept, narrative and sequential art. Since graduating she has continued on as a freelancer, developing graphics, concept art, comics and book illustrations for various clients, with The Critter Family: The Fun Begins! being the first published children's book her artwork was being featured in.

# About the Author

Barbara ventured into storytelling to encourage young people to read for entertainment. She crafted her stories to help young readers determine fact from fiction. She gives children an opportunity to reference links at the end of the book. Barbara finds learning to be a lifetime experience and hopes children read more as a form of entertainment!

Made in United States
North Haven, CT
10 April 2023

35277859R00057